More Maritime Mysteries

everyone has a story

Bill Jessome

NIMBUS
PUBLISHING

For Frank and Betty Avruch of Newton Center, Ma.
…We go way back—back fifty years…
And still talking.
And for Dave and Audrey Wright of Barrie, On
…also special people.

＊

Nimbus Publishing Limited
PO Box 9166
Halifax, NS B3K 5M8
(902) 455-4286

Printed and bound in Canada
Designer: Margaret Issenman, MGDC

Canadian Cataloguing in Publication Data
    Jessome, Bill
    More maritime mysteries: everyone has a story

    ISBN 1-55109-379-0

1. Ghosts—Maritime Provinces. 2. Tales—Maritime Provinces. I. Title.
GR113.5.M37J473 2001   398.2'0971505   C2001-902178-X

We acknowledge the financial support of the Government of Canada through the Book Publishing Industry Development Program (BPIDP) and the Canada Council for our publishing activities.

Table of Contents

Introduction

Not a ghost of a chance will I write another *Maritime Mysteries* book.

Well, that was my immediate response when asked if there was going to be another ghost book. My concern was that, like movies, the sequel is rarely as good as the original and there is disappointment all around. However, the response was so overwhelming following the publication of the first book—*Maritime Mysteries and the Ghosts Who Surround Us*—that I decided to tackle a second book with fingers crossed that it might be as well-received as the first one.

Most of these stories came to me from hither and yon, by way of mail and the electronic highways, by chance meetings in shopping centres, on the streets of the Maritimes, in movie houses, and even in church. I am indebted to those who have a story to tell and I'm most grateful that they told them to me. So let's go a-haunting.

For Alf & Judy
Enjoy
Bill Jessome

Chapter One

Unwanted Houseguests and Haunted Homesteads

Τhat Τhing in the Attic

I shall call her Sarah Ives, and this ghostly encounter happened while Sarah was on a weekend getaway in a small community on Nova Scotia's western shore.

Sarah was given the keys to a two-hundred-year-old ramshackle house by a close friend. She intended to spend the entire weekend doing absolutely nothing but sleeping and catching up on her reading.

There were three bedrooms on the second floor, but she continued her exploration of the house down the long, narrow hall to three steps and a door. The door opened to a narrow passageway and another closed door. A rush of cold air swept over her when she opened it, but she was delighted to find a smaller bedroom with a spectacular view of the Bay of Fundy. Sure, the room was cold compared to the rest of the house, but the stunning vista made up for it.

The room was sparsely furnished with a bit of a Victorian gloom about it. It didn't take a huge stretch of imagination to see it as dark, foreboding even. To her delight, though, the bed was enormous with a large head and footboard. Sarah could imagine Queen Victoria sitting up in such a bed with a white shawl covering her royal head. The small dresser had a cracked mirror and when she passed it, Sarah stuck her tongue out and laughed at her own distorted image. The floor was a series of uneven boards that creaked when you walked over them.

After supper and a shower, Sarah retired early and welcomed the sleep that came quickly but wouldn't last.

Something woke her in the dark. A sound perhaps? Or was it a dream? She stared into the gloom. The house was still. Not a sound anywhere.

Then she heard what had awakened her—a clawing, scratching sound along the footboard of the bed that spoke of slow and deliberate movement. By the shaft of moonlight coming through the window, she thought she could make out a form. Sarah froze, paralyzed with fright. The sound moved closer, around the bed, carrying with it a horrible smell. Sarah tried to scream but no sound came out of her throat.

The face that moved into the light was a sickening greyish-green, framed by white, lifeless hair. Boney hands reached for her with fingertips like black claws, wrapping around Sarah's throat and squeezing. Instead of pressure, Sarah felt a terrible coldness around her neck. The face pressed close to Sarah's cheek, and the horrible lips parted, uttering a babble of unintelligible words.

In a panic, Sarah reached for the lamp and the thing shrank back from the light, covering its face and passing through the wall.

Sarah stumbled out of bed, grabbed some clothes, and left the house immediately. But doubts followed her away from that place. Had it been real? Just a dream, a nightmare? She had to know. Dawn was breaking as Sarah turned the car around.

The house was just as she had left it. She slowly climbed the stairs to the attic and, holding her breath, stepped inside. Her eyes swept the room, looking for some indication that she was or wasn't dreaming. The fluttering curtains caught Sarah's eye. A draft? The window was shut tight. She saw no one, but knew she wasn't alone. As Sarah raced downstairs to the outside world, a horrible stench chased after her.

The Ghost in the Grist Mill

There was a grist mill on Prince Edward Island owned by a Mr. Scott. His was a thriving business and he was considered one of the best mill operators in the province. However, the hand of misfortune struck the family in the form of a mysterious illness that laid everyone low. No one in the family was able to operate the mill and Mr. Scott was concerned about the back orders waiting to be processed.

One late evening the miller was awakened by the familiar sounds of machinery in the mill. Not knowing what was going on, Mr. Scott made his way outside to the mill. He moved cautiously toward the half-open door, pushed it all the way open with the tips of his fingers, and went inside. No one was there, but the bags were filled with flour. Mystified, he heard footsteps coming down from around the machinery, but could see no one. He followed the sound of the footsteps to the stacked bags of ground flour, and witnessed something that shook him to his very soul. He saw flour being sifted through invisible fingers! Suddenly the machinery stopped and the lights went out.

Mr. Scott turned the lights on and waited, but no one was there. Just before locking up, the mill owner looked once more at the sacks of flour and wondered—milled by whom? Or what?

The Inside, Outside Ghosts

A trip to Windsor, Nova Scotia would not be complete without a visit to Haliburton House Museum where, if you're lucky, you'll bump into the ghost of Thomas Chandler Haliburton himself. Of Loyalist descent, this famous Nova Scotian was born in Windsor in 1796. He became a politician and jurist, but he's more famous as the author of *Sam Slick the Yankee Peddler*.

Inside Haliburton estate—also known as Clifton Place—the ghost of Thomas Chandler Haliburton sits in his room in his favourite easy chair. He's deep in conversation with someone who, according to some, could be an old political friend and foe, Joseph Howe.

Haliburton may have loved Nova Scotia, but he loved England more and moved there in the mid-1850s. In 1865, he died at the age of 69, and was buried in a cemetery along the Thames River. His body may have been buried in England but apparently his spirit came home—home to Windsor, Nova Scotia.

As you explore the grounds of Clifton Place, another ghost may cross your path. He's a young soldier of the Black Watch known to local folk as the Lone Piper. There are several versions of what caused the piper's death, but as far as young maidens were and are concerned, there is only one explanation—lost love.

While the young piper and his regiment were passing through Windsor on their way to Annapolis Royale, they bivouacked near the Haliburton property. The young soldier and his sweetheart met near a pond on the estate, where he told his love that he was being shipped back to England. Unable to imagine life without him, she jumped into the pond and drowned. The distraught soldier, on seeing her ghostly reflection in the water, joined her in everlasting sleep.

Legend has it that if young maidens dance thirteen times around Piper's Pond, as it became known, the waters will give life back to the young lovers. Some people say that if you really listen, you can hear the faint sounds of the pipes.

The Trenton Poltergeist

Not far from Blue Mountain, we find another ghostly tale. This one happened in the town of Trenton to the household of a woman we'll call Mary. The lives of Mary and her family were forever changed the moment they stepped inside their new home on Maple Street.

Once they were settled in, the family noticed that all the windows were nailed shut. But were they sealed to keep someone out, or someone or something in?

Questions but no answers—that is, until night fell. No sooner was the family in bed than ungodly things began happening. One after the other the nailed-down windows flew open and slammed shut again. Every door in the house opened and slammed. The family checked the windows in the morning only to find that they were still nailed tightly shut.

In days to come, there were more unexplained happenings. Objects flew through the rooms. The kettle, with steam coming from its spout, would float up to the ceiling and come down again on its own. The fire in the stove would go out for no reason whatsoever, and no one in the house was able to relight it. The fire would start up on its own.

There was one bedroom that was so cold nobody could sleep in it. Mary tried to keep the door open by propping a chair against it, but as soon as it was secured, the door would slam shut and the chair would go flying across the room against the far wall. One day Mary was late getting home from shopping and arrived to find her children waiting outside for her, too afraid to go back inside. As you can imagine, keeping babysitters was a problem. They never came back a second time.

The final straw came when Mary arrived home one evening to find her husband and five children huddled together in the kitchen. He told his wife, "That's it, we're moving."

And they did, keeping their fingers crossed that the poltergeist didn't decide to go with them. Some time later, Mary happened to meet the new tenant who told her that while watching television, the children and her husband saw a dog walking across the living room. When her husband went after the dog, it faded before his very eyes. They moved, too. Everyone does.

The Ghost of Egan House

*B*ehind the walls of 2776 Dutch Village Road, another Maritime Mystery unfolds. If you can be lured with a story of lost love and a ghostly bride that never reached the altar, join me in a journey down a dark corridor of time to west-end Halifax and a place known as Egan House.

I made my way to that old west-end landmark and looked up at the impressive structure, feeling a deep sadness for the young woman who, according to legend, died on the eve of her wedding. What caused her death, no one knows. Still, her ghost has been seen wandering the second floor wearing a wedding dress—one can only surmise that she wore that dress to the grave and back!

But when I stepped inside Egan House, I encountered no apparitions hiding in dark corridors, no musty smells, no unholy screams coming from the cellar or attic.

Back in the Victorian era, the property was known as Rockwood Place and it was home to a three-storey wooden structure. Unfortunately, a chimney spark set fire to Rockwood Place and the top floor and roof were destroyed. A newspaper account of the day reported that just a week earlier, city council had recommended that the property be purchased for use as an inebriated home (today, they're referred to as detox centers). In 1891, Halifax could have bought Rockwood for a mere $8,900.

After the fire, Rockwood estate was bought by Captain William H. Smith, chairman of the board of examiners of masters and mates. When Captain Smith died in 1906, his widow sold Rockwood. The land was divided into two sections and purchased by two families who were related. One section was bought by a Daniel Chisholm, who was in the lumber business, and the other by Thomas J. Egan, a gunsmith and sporting goods dealer. The Chisholm family lived there until 1946 and the Egan family well into the 1960s. Daniel Chisholm's son Thomas is the grandson of Thomas J. Egan, and holding steady at 98 years as of this writing. Mr. Chisholm told me that his old homestead was eventually torn down and in its place the present Municipal Building stands. When I suggested to this fine old gentleman that the Egan home may be haunted, he told me I'd been informed by someone with a vivid imagination. Be that as it may, this is what was told to me.

At the time of this writing, Egan House is occupied by the Halifax Regional Municipality and the old home is cluttered with modern technology. I had a strong feeling that the old and the new did not blend well and I wondered how the ghost felt about the twenty-first-century intrusion.

I was accompanied upstairs by Ruth McCulloch, administrative assistant to the director of public works and transportation. Ruth has yet to see the ghost but admitted that other people have. Ruth told me of an unsuspecting carpenter doing renovations, unaware of the resident ghost. The only people in the house at the time were the workers. Something compelled the carpenter to shift his gaze upstairs where he saw, standing on the landing and wearing a wedding dress, the ghost of a young woman.

During another incident, an employee seeking privacy made his way to the attic to study important documents. He settled himself at a large conference table, glad for the peace and quiet, but could not rid himself of a strong feeling that he was not alone in the room. The hair on the back of his neck stood up with the sensation of cold air sweeping past him. Another employee was passing a second floor office when she noticed a young woman seated by the window. When she went back to check, the woman was gone.

There were many more incidents. An employee complained that he couldn't get his work done because he was distracted by someone who kept passing his open door. Even more distracting was the discovery that nobody was there. More frightening than most of the encounters, an employee was working in the computer room when she felt a cold spot near her. Suddenly she lost control of her hands, which seemed to move on their own. As if guided by an external force, her hands reached out towards the cold spot. Her trembling fingers encircled what seemed to be a human form!

As the haunting unfolded, staff members were told it was the spirit of a young woman who died on the eve of her wedding and was buried in her wedding dress. The spirit of this young woman has most often been seen on the second floor, and it is believed her bedroom was at the top of the stairs facing Dutch Village Road.

As Ruth and I made our way to the second floor, I caught a whiff of lavender. Perhaps it was only my imagination. Hmmm. We stood for a moment or two on the second floor next to the ghost's bedroom, waiting and listening. But there was no energy force, not even a sweep of cold air. Only an emptiness.

As I left, I wondered if the ghost of Egan House existed at all. If she hadn't been an Egan or a relative, who then? It's a Maritime Mystery, to be sure.

Outside, I stood on the sidewalk staring at the upstairs window of that little bedroom. It is said that from the street she has been seen sitting in the window. But not on this day, and not for me.

The DuBury Ghosts

She said, "Everyone knows the DuBury house is haunted."

Well, I didn't know. Didn't know, that is, until a letter arrived by way of a local bookstore. The letter was from Mrs. Marion Sponagle of Goldboro, Nova Scotia. Marion Sponagle lived in the DuBury home in the seventies and early eighties, and experienced several unexplained occurrences while living there.

The ghost house in question was built by Count Robert DuBury, Belgium's Vice Council, in 1873, and is located on Main Street in Saint John, New Brunswick. DuBury was an engineer by profession, one of the builders of Canada's railroads. He married Lucy Simonds of the trading post family whom he met while both were attending university in Germany. They raised nine children, though some argue it was thirteen.

Marion's first encounter could be described as a forerunner. One morning a visiting friend complained about a severe cold spot that seemed to surround him. The elderly gentleman told Marion he was tired and felt ill, and asked her to take him home immediately. Just then, the clock chimed the hour and a bell began to ring inexplicably. Marion remembers telling him, "It tolls for thee." Exactly one week later, her friend was found dead.

The second incident happened while Marion was dusting the stairs. She heard the mysterious sounds of footsteps and a child's laughter coming up the stairs behind her. When she turned around there was no one there.

One day, she heard someone coming in the house through the sun porch. Thinking it was her son and grandson, she went to check but there was no one in the house but herself. Mrs. Sponagle also had to deal with a cold spot in her bedroom. Time after time, she was forced to move her bed in order to avoid the icy chill. For those who are not aware, a cold spot is a sure sign that a ghost is nearby, perhaps standing over your bed or chair.

Marion Sponagle was not the only person who had to deal with the ghost of DuBury house. Ken Spink lived in the home in the mid-eighties and had his share of ghostly encounters. At the time, the house was divided into two apartments, and Mr. Spink lived on the first floor. While relaxing one evening with his canine companion at his feet, in a room that was at one time the office of Count DuBury, he heard a swishing sound. The dog's body arched, and the hairs on its back bristled. The dog slunk away as the swishing came closer and closer to where Mr. Spink was seated. There was no visible sign of anyone else in the room. Ken was aware that the presence paused, standing behind his chair, and he felt a breath of cold air on the back of his neck. Ken was reminded of the sound that a floor-length crinoline makes when a woman moves, before the sound and presence faded away.

Ken also recalls his second-floor tenant complaining that every morning she would find her expensive print on the floor. Mr. Spink checked to make sure the painting was properly secured and told his tenant that there was no earthly reason the picture should fall. The next morning the tenant again found the print on the floor.

Why the haunting? Well, the DuBurys were famous for giving parties. According to legend, a woman attending one of the parties made her way upstairs to one of the bedrooms and hanged herself. Perhaps she's the ghost that haunts DuBury house. But who is the little child on the stairs?

Another Maritime Mystery to ponder during those sleepless nights.

Lights Out

*F*ishermen sailing past Barachois Head depend on the light at Port Bickerton, Nova Scotia to guide them into safe waters, but there was a time when the light didn't burn so brightly. Some force other than human hands kept turning the light off. Was the lighthouse haunted by the ghost of a drowned fisherman? We'll never know. Today the restored Port Bickerton lighthouse is used as an interpretation centre for all provincial lighthouses.

Back in the fifties, assistant lighthouse keeper Jim Johnson wondered if he was sharing the lighthouse with a ghost.

Jim vividly remembers a few peculiarities that would lead one to believe in the paranormal. One cold and bright February evening, Jim saw a beam of light from a vehicle or someone carrying a lantern coming down along the beach toward the lighthouse. Whatever it was, it left not a wheel track nor a single footprint in the snow. Jim also remembers the first time the light in the tower was turned off by some unnatural means. It was just before dusk, when Jim went up to the tower to fill the oil tank and clean the glass and wick. After lighting the wick, Jim closed the hatch to the tower as well as the one outside. Both hatches were securely locked by a deadbolt. He went back down to the living quarters where he continued his duties. Sometimes in the late evening, he'd work on his model ships or listen to shortwave radio.

On one of these evenings the lighthouse keeper, an avid horseshoe player, got into his dune buggy and headed up the beach to play in the local horseshoe tournament. It wasn't long before he came racing back to the lighthouse screaming to his assistant, "Why didn't you light the light?"

Jim assured him that he had. Both made their way up to the tower to find that both hatches were open and the light had been turned off by someone—or something.

The lighthouse keeper, shaking his head in bewilderment, returned to finish the tournament and Jim returned to the tower every half hour to check on the light. A couple of hours after the first incident, it happened again, but this time the light only dimmed. Someone had turned down the wick. Jim raced back to the tower to find the hatches open and the light in the lamp flickering.

Another evening Jim noticed a light coming down the beach toward the lighthouse. Thinking it was a member of the lighthouse keeper's family, Jim awakened his boss. With flashlights in hand, they went to meet whomever it was. The only thing they saw was the mysterious light coming down the beach. In the morning they checked but could not find any tracks—human or otherwise.

To this very day, Jim Johnson can offer no explanation of what came down the beach that night, or who turned off the light in the tower. A haunted lighthouse? Why not?

The Spirits of Christmas Past

This is the story of a Scottish family who left the old land for New Scotland. Not long after their arrival, they moved into what was then known as the John Kelly Farm, located at the head of River Hebert, Nova Scotia. Was the old farm haunted? You decide.

There were five in the Emslie family—Alex, his wife Ira, and their three children, Lexie, Alastair, and Nancy. Nancy Huston is the family member who brought this Christmas story to my attention.

It was Christmas Eve, 1929 when the first incident occurred. The house was quite far off the main road, so the mailman would call the Emslie family whenever there was mail. On this particular Christmas Eve, he called to let them know Santa had left several gifts in their mailbox. The children, anxious to find out what Santa had left, begged their father to let them hurry up the lane to fetch the mail. The father lit the lantern for ten-year-old Lexie and eight-year-old Alex, who set off up the long winding lane to the mailbox. The parents watched their children disappear around a bend in the lane and stayed at the window, anxiously waiting for their safe return.

Finally they saw a light coming down the lane. As the light came closer they saw a man carrying a lantern walking between their children. He wore heavy work socks over his pants. Mr. Emslie went to the door to greet the stranger while his wife went to the kitchen to make tea. When he opened the door to invite the stranger in, there was no one there but his two children carrying several packages. When the father asked his children who had accompanied them, they replied somewhat puzzled, "There was no one with us."

The father took the lantern and went outside to check for himself. When he returned, he told his wife, "Only the bairn's tracks, lass." In time, the incident was forgotten.

A year passed and once again it was Christmas Eve. The fire burned brightly and the Emslie home smelled of fir and baking. As darkness fell, the family heard sleighbells coming down the lane. When they went to the window, they saw a horse-drawn sleigh skimming over the snow. Alex Emslie told his wife that he would go greet whomever it was and stable the horse. With a lantern to guide him, he stepped outside to be greeted only by the cold night air. There was not a trace of horse, sleigh, or driver anywhere.

When winter passed, the Emslie family moved from the John Kelly farm.

Alex and Ira Emslie passed over to the other side. As of this writing, Alastair lives in Pugwash, Nova Scotia, Lexie in British Columbia, and Nancy in Dartmouth.

Oh, a Christmas thought: If you hear the sound of sleighbells coming down your lane this Christmas Eve, take heart. Merry Christmas to all and to all a good night.

A Too-Frisky Spirit

*T*he lady introduced herself as Mrs. Anonymous. It seems she had a problem with a ghost who liked her a little too much.

The first incident happened about a month after she and her husband bought a new place. Actually, the house was not new at all. It was quite old, but it was large and stood on a high cliff overlooking the ocean. They thought it was gothic and romantic. When I asked where it was, she merely smiled and went on with her story.

"My husband was away on business when it happened. The kids were in bed and I had just retired when I felt a wave-motion rolling across the mattress. Then there was this cool air on my neck. It felt as if someone was lying next to me. I froze. Didn't know what to do. Then when I felt a coolness slowly moving up my thigh I flew out of bed and spent the rest of the night on the sofa downstairs. That's where I slept until my husband returned. When I told him what had happened, he started to laugh until he saw the look on my face, then like a typical husband, shouted, 'I'll shoot him on sight!'

"When I made inquiries about the history of the place, I was told that a husband shot and killed a handsome young sea captain he'd caught in the arms of his wife. When I thanked my local historian, he smiled and said, 'Is he up to his old tricks again?'

"We moved but even now when I'm about to get in bed, I wonder if there's a pair of invisible arms waiting to embrace me."

Stop Haunting Me!

*T*his amazing haunting is happening in a home in Marion Bridge, Cape Breton. Mary Buchanan Beaton and her family bought the home on Trout Brook Road in Marion Bridge more than five years ago. Everyone in the family was enjoying the new surroundings until one morning when Mrs. Beaton felt something pass by in the hall. She's unable to explain exactly what it was, as she didn't see anything.

She said, "It's more like a presence, an energy than anything else."

That wasn't the case with her five-year-old son Buchanan, who not only sees the ghost, but talks and argues with it as well. Her son told her that the ghost's name is Mia and that she constantly follows and harasses him.

The first time Mia made her presence known was while young Buchanan was asleep. His mother heard screams coming from his bedroom and when she rushed upstairs, she found her son sitting up in bed screaming, "Go, go! I don't want you here!" When Mrs. Beaton asked who he was talking to, Buchanan told her it was Mia and she was bothering him. He asked his mother to tell Mia to go. Mrs. Beaton knew it wasn't his imaginary friend because *its* name was Billie.

There were times when young Buchanan tried to control Mia by telling her to get in the closet. He'd close the door, thinking that would be that. But no sooner would he return to doing what children do, than she would be standing next to him or sitting in the rocker.

Most nerve-wracking of all was an afternoon when Mrs. Beaton and Buchanan were about to leave in the car. Buchanan refused to get in the car, demanding that his mother tell Mia she couldn't come. Mrs. Beaton looked around, but could see no one but her son. To pacify him, she scolded Mia severely and told her she couldn't come along, and to go back in the house immediately. But while driving down the highway, Buchanan began screaming that Mia was sitting next to him. The mother had no choice but to turn the car around and go back.

Mrs. Beaton's three-year-old deaf daughter is also haunted by the ghost. Occasionally she would cry and point at something close to her.

Mrs. Buchanan's then-husband didn't believe in ghosts, but found out the hard way. One day he arrived home to find the place empty. He called out to see if anyone was home and heard a strange voice answer. He thought perhaps some member of the family was down in the basement so down he went and again asked if anyone was there.

The same strange voice answered back.

Which brings us to Mia. Who is she and where did she come from? Mrs. Beaton's sister Lisa was asked by a friend at a party, "How is your sister Mary getting along with the ghost?"

When pressed, he told Lisa that during a summer camp years ago some of the children asked the camp supervisors the name of the strange-looking little girl playing with them. Was Mia also a summer camp girl many years ago, perhaps drowned in the Mira River?

In her search for the answers to these haunting questions, Mrs. Beaton found out that a long, long time ago, a young girl died in a snowstorm near the camp and the Beaton home. Is Mia merely attempting to find her way back home through the living? Perhaps through young Buchanan?

Mary Buchanan Beaton is becoming concerned that one day Mia may cause serious harm to her children and she wants the ghost of Mia out of their home and out of their lives.

Spooked

With today's congested traffic, what human wouldn't be afraid to cross the road? But why would a ghost be afraid?

According to Mrs. Jean Tavanaee of Bridgetown, Nova Scotia ghosts are definitely afraid to cross the road. Here is Mrs. Tavanaee's explanation.

A peddler was given a room for the night in a home near Chester and sometime during the evening, someone sneaked into his room and murdered him.

It wasn't long after that the ghost of the murdered peddler returned to the home where this foul deed was committed, and he wreaked havoc on those who lived in the house. He made his ghostly presence known by hurling pots and pans across the kitchen floor. There wasn't a door or window that remained closed. He roamed and prowled all hours of the night. It got so bad that the owners didn't know what they were going to do. That is, until someone told them ghosts don't like to travel and under no circumstances will they cross the road. The owners gave up the old homestead to the ghost and built a home across the road. Seemed to work. They were never again bothered by that miserable old spirit.

The Maitland Ghosts

*A*s if one ghost roaming around your property isn't enough, how about three? Up in Maitland where the Shubenacadie River and the Bay of Fundy meet, there's a beautiful old home that was built in 1850 by local shipbuilder Archibald McCallum. The home had changed hands a couple of times before Kim and Brian Van de Vrie fixed their eyes on it. When it became available, they grabbed it— spooks and all. These two enterprising people knew that the location on the Shubie shore was ideal for a river rafting business. So what about the ghosts?

Well, according to legend, a servant was mysteriously murdered on the third floor and on the anniversary of his death, blood stains appear on that exact spot. Although she has not yet seen the manifestations herself, Kim Van de Vrie says some of the former owners have seen the blood on the floor, and her sister-in-law and a housesitter have met the ghost of the murdered servant. The locals who know the history of the McCallum home usually stay away. If they do go inside, they avoid going upstairs.

A Maritime Mystery that still remains unexplained is the woman in white who has been seen walking along the Shubie shore in back of the home. To this day, no one has made contact with her or uncovered any records of a drowning or murder on the Shubenacadie. Kim Van de Vrie tells the story of a curse put on the home and family back in the 1800s. A vessel tied up at the local wharf one night, and the mate and some crew members trucked up to the house to ask if they could replenish their supply of fresh water. When they were refused, the mate placed a curse on the family and the water, causing the well water to become contaminated. To this very day, those who live in the house use spring and bottled water only.

Is Kim Van de Vrie afraid of what's living in and outside her beautiful home? Not in the least. She says, "Let the wind howl and the floors creak..."

She loves it...spooks and all!

The Ghost of Ol' Charlie

*A*ccording to Wayne MacAulay of New Glasgow, his father couldn't pass up a good deal when he saw one. But there was a catch.

There was an old house in Westville, Nova Scotia that the owner wanted to get rid of. He was so desperate, he was ready to let it go for fifty dollars. Whoever bought it would have to move it or tear it down piece by piece and take it as far away from the owner as possible. Mr. MacAulay had the fifty dollars all right and yes, that was his intention—tear it down and rebuild it in another town.

The owner was no doubt relieved, but being an honest Pictonian, told MacAulay, "You'll never live in that house."

"Oh, and why is that?" MacAulay inquired.

"Because," said the owner, "it's haunted."

"Well," said MacAulay, "It'll have to get along with me, or get out."

So, Wayne's father and uncle tore the old haunted house down to its foundation and moved it to a site in Priestville where Wayne's mother still lives to this day —with a ghost by the name of Ol' Charlie. Incidentally, Charlie is partial to the ladies—if he gets the chance, he'll let them know just how with a friendly pat as they pass by.

One night when Wayne went to bed, the covers suddenly lifted and wrapped around his head. Wayne struggled and struggled to free himself. When he finally got the covers off his head, he jumped out of bed and turned the lights on. But when he checked the room and under the bed, there was no one there but himself. Wayne spent the rest of the night on the sofa downstairs.

In the morning when he told his parents and brother, they only laughed and said it was just Ol' Charlie. That night he took all the blankets and tucked them tightly under his body. It didn't work. They were torn from him and ended up at the foot of the bed. Wayne made three attempts to keep the blankets under his arm, but each time they were yanked from him. That was the last time Wayne ever slept in his parents' home. As far as he knows, Charlie is still there keeping his mother company, as well as any other lady that happens to drop in.

The Ghost in the Cellar

For some people, owning a haunted house is a great conversation piece during dinner. Others, on discovering that their just-purchased dream house is haunted, put a For Sale sign out front and leave. It's another matter entirely when the haunting is in a business establishment.

While lunching at The Cellar, a popular eatery in Bedford, Nova Scotia, I was approached by hostess Earlene Barrington who whispered in my ear, "This place is haunted. I'll be back with the proof." A few minutes later the restaurant's bookkeeper Joanne Dolan sat across from me and hesitantly told me more about the restaurant and the strange occurrences therein.

Back in the late 1800s the honourable James Butler of Fort Sackville, a member of the legislative council, operated a farm on the site where The Cellar restaurant now stands. Supposedly, a woman was murdered there one dark night, and her spirit haunts the place to this day. The farm is long gone, and today those pristine pastures have given way to the fast food emporiums and gas stations that line the banks of the Sackville River.

I must confess that I can remember feeling uncomfortable while using the bathroom facilities located in the basement, or in this case, the cellar. It was as if someone was nearby—watching. But this is not my ghost story, it's Joanne Dolan's.

When Joanne first realized that the restaurant was haunted, she was in her office working. Suddenly the room became very cold and when she looked up, a mist shaped like a white body floated past her. Joanne watched it until it vanished. She stood up, shook the cold wave and fear from her body, and immediately left the office to find out if other employees had experienced any strange happenings.

They had. There had been times when office furniture and restaurant supplies were moved and, as if by an invisible hand, the ceiling fan, cash registers, and computers were turned on and off. The chef and kitchen staff witnessed strange things such as pots levitating, then crashing to the floor. Some of the employees, cleaning up after the restaurant closed, reported hearing a voice from the cellar calling their names. The waiters didn't check, they didn't have to. They knew who it was.

One afternoon while Joanne was down in the cellar, the air in the room became icy cold and an equally cold hand touched her shoulder. When she turned around, there was nobody there and she realized it was a phantom presence. She stood up, looked around the room, and in a shaky voice asked it to leave her alone. There was no response, but as she went back up the stairs the air in the room became warm again.

Now, when I have lunch at the restaurant, I'm forced to steal a glance at the cellar entrance. I'm wondering if the ghost is standing in the doorway—watching!

A Holy Spirit

As told by Margaret Powell

This ghost story happened in England many years ago. The Maritime Mystery connection? The author now lives in our Maritime community, and we don't know for certain whether the ghost followed her to Nova Scotia, or if he's still searching for her in England. It seems that the ghost was spiritually and emotionally attached to the lady in question.

This true ghost story happened to Mrs. Margaret Powell, who now lives in Bedford, Nova Scotia. It began when the Powell family bought a seven-hundred-year-old farm in Oxfordshire, England. At one time the farmhouse had been a monastery. In that ancient place, perhaps since the seventeenth century, wandered the ghost of a monk. I say three hundred years because John Powell, the son of our storyteller, believes from his research that the monk was perhaps murdered by one of Oliver Cromwell's soldiers in the early 1640s when the first civil war in England began.

In any event, this is what Margaret told me about living with a spirit, a religious one, at that.

"I remember one evening when I was entertaining some friends and I was going from the living room to the dining room into the kitchen. The dining room door was very wide, you could drive one of those small English cars through it. Well, I could not get through that door even though it was wide open. I stepped back and said, 'oh!' Whatever was blocking my way stepped aside and I could go into the kitchen.

"Many, many times after that incident I would go out and see a shape in a robe with a cowl over its head. I could never see his face. He was definitely a monk. Often I would see him standing there and I always spoke to him. I always said 'good morning' or 'good evening' and I was never really afraid of him. I'd walk right past him and I would also let him know when we were having company.

"One night I was sitting knitting a sweater for one of the children. My back was to the fireplace and you know when a draught comes down the chimney, a lot of smoke comes out. Well, I was sitting there and at the time I had long hair and I had taken it down and left it loose. Suddenly my hair blew across my face, but there was no smoke. I didn't say anything because the children were there and I didn't want to scare them.

"I remember one particular morning I couldn't sleep so I got up and went downstairs to make myself a cup of tea. Well, you went down the stairs a ways and then there was a landing where the stairs continued down the other way. I got to the landing and he was standing there and I stood there looking at him and he was looking at me. Then he began to disappear. I put my hands behind my back and bent over to watch him vanish straight down through the floor! Another morning, I wasn't feeling well and my husband went down to the kitchen to make a cup of tea. Now, the attic in the house was only floored half way; you couldn't just walk from one end of the attic to the other. I heard footsteps and thought my husband was coming up the stairs with my tea. Well whoever it was walked the full length of the house across the attic floor that wasn't there.

"The morning we left the house for the last time, I was sitting in the window seat in the dining room holding the children's cricket bats, our umbrellas, and walking sticks. One walking stick was my husband's and the other had been given to me by a sea captain. It had an ivory handle. I had everything tied in three places, the top, middle and bottom. Suddenly my walking stick, not my husband's, came straight out of the tied bundle straight up in the air and flew across the dining room floor and broke two pieces of ivory out of the handle. The monk, of course, was upset I was leaving and I said to him, 'I shall be back to see you.'

"I came back after the new people moved in. I went into this particular room and I told him, 'I'm going this time, but I tell you I'll be back.' I could feel he was there. I couldn't see him, but I could feel he was standing there listening...watching."

Mrs. Powell ended our visit by telling me that she has felt strange things and known events that were yet to happen.

One night Mrs. Powell awakened and told her husband there was trouble at home in England. "But don't worry," she told him, "it's not your family, it's mine."

He asked what she meant by that, and she answered, "Well, in my dream there were two tombstones on the balcony, and they both had hangman's nooses on them. One was full and rustling in the wind and the other was rustling also but there was nothing in it. It's my family, not yours."

Two weeks later, a letter arrived informing Mrs. Powell that her sister-in-law's father, a farmer, had died.

And there's more, she tells us: "Two weeks before my husband died I told the administrator of my building, 'You must put this information on file.' She wanted to know why, and I told her that if something happened to one of us, to contact the funeral people listed in the information who have all the instructions and know exactly what to do. Within two weeks, my husband was gone."

The Ghost of Waterloo Row

*H*ow many times have you walked down your street without giving your surroundings a second thought? Perhaps you Frederictonians have walked by several old mansions in the city and thought them stately, but harmless, old residences. Think again— one's haunted!

Maurice Cormier, a retired government worker, was told about the haunting by an associate who once rented an apartment in the mansion in question. The house is located on Waterloo Row in Fredericton, New Brunswick. The landlord who bought the home intended to turn it into as many small apartments as possible, planning to keep expenses down by doing the renovations himself.

While working late one night he decided to sleep over so he could get an early start in the morning. During the night he was awakened by a noise upstairs. Half awake, he got out of bed and followed the noise, but was stopped dead by the sight of a woman carrying a lantern. Before the landlord could collect his wits enough to ask who she was and what she was doing there, she walked straight through the wall!

In the days that followed, the landlord decided to tear down that same wall on the third floor to build another small apartment. To his surprise, when he removed the wallboard he discovered a door leading into a bedroom. It was the exact spot in the wall where the ghost with the lantern had disappeared.

So, next time you're strolling down your street, take nothing for granted. Remember, as you go by some of those stately old mansions, that lifeless eyes may be watching you pass.

Ghost House

There's a house in Digby County that is haunted from the cellar to the attic. The owners had it with the overbearing spirit and the home, as of this writing, is empty and up for sale. The owners do not want the exact location published, for obvious reasons. I met the daughter of the owner during a reading of my *Maritime Mysteries* book at the Maritime Museum of the Atlantic. I'll call her Lidia.

The house in question has managed to stand against the elements and man's penchant for tearing things down for over a century and a half, and the ghost that haunts the place may be just as old. In 1987 the family, having Maritime roots, decided to leave Ontario and come back to Nova Scotia to stay. They were looking for an older and larger home that could be turned into a bed and breakfast. They found exactly what they were looking for. The house needed a lot of work but it had excellent potential, and with a lot of time, sweat, and effort, they brought the home back to its original state. Still, the B&B concept never materialized nor did the home become a permanent residence for the family, for very good reason.

It wasn't very long after they moved in that they realized the place was haunted. The first incident occurred while the father was at work and Lidia and her sister were in school. While doing her household chores, the mother was suddenly startled by a loud explosion coming from somewhere upstairs. Thinking it might be an old bookcase in Lidia's bedroom, the mother went up to investigate but found nothing disturbed. On the way downstairs she heard another loud noise.

This time it seemed like it was coming from the basement. While making her way down the basement steps, she felt uneasy and a fear overwhelmed her. She felt there was something or someone close by. As she cautiously made her way down the cellar steps, the heel of her right shoe caught on a protruding nail and she fell forward. Before she toppled headfirst down the stairs, however, a pressure like a pair of strong hands stopped her fall. The strange occurrence convinced her that something else was occupying their home.

Things were normal until a few weeks later when the mother heard footsteps and laughter that sounded like children running up and down the back stairs though there was no one in the house but herself. When she went to check, the sounds of children playing stopped.

The family wondered if they should stay or leave. The decision was made one evening during the father's nightly security check of the house. His wife and daughters were asleep and everything appeared normal as he made his way upstairs, turning off the lights on the way. Normal, that is, until he got in bed. Suddenly there was a moaning or crying coming from one of the bedrooms. Thinking it might be his daughter's cat, he went to her room to check. The cat and his daughter were fast asleep. He returned to his room and got back in bed. No sooner was he in bed than the moaning started again. It was louder this time and seemed to come into his bedroom and stop at the foot of the bed. Distressing, but it was the next development that nearly frightened him out of his wits—the moaning was now coming from his sleeping wife! That was the final straw. The family packed up and moved to Halifax.

Strangely, the mother still visits the house to check on its condition and unwelcome inhabitants. As of this writing, it's still empty. No buyers. I think they know who lives there!

A Halloween Dare

When I was growing up, my friends and I participated in some awfully scary dares. One of our favourites involved tying someone to a tombstone on Halloween night. We'd hide behind other tombstones and wait to see how long our victim could stay tied before screaming to be cut loose. Those childish games bring to mind a Halloween "I Dare You" story that I heard many years ago.

The haunted house stood empty for years and nobody really knew who or what was haunting it. Some said a family member was found hanged in one of the bedrooms. A boy and girl—let's call them Mikie and Leah—accepted a dare from their friends to stay inside the house until midnight. To make sure they didn't come down with a case of cold feet, their friends promised they would watch from a safe distance away.

Under a full moon, the boys and girls rode their bicycles two miles out of town to the haunted house. On their arrival, they found an ideal vantage point behind a huge stump fence that was located directly across the road. Once more the rules of the dare were set down, as the older boys and girls expected Mikie and Leah to back out at the last minute. But the duo stood their ground and convinced themselves that there were no such things as ghosts. Mikie was always ready for adventure. Leah, on the other hand, was somewhat reluctant, but it was much too late in the game to chicken out. At the appointed hour, they climbed over the fence and set off across the gravel road, unsure of what might be waiting for them.

The house was set back some distance from the road. An overgrowth of grass and weeds covered most of the path that led up to the porch. To the left of the path, a giant dogwood cast an eerie shadow on the house. When Mikie and Leah reached the bottom step they stopped and stared up at the front door. Were they seeing things or was that a face staring back at them?

With a pounding heart, Leah followed Mikie up the steps. It was now or never. Mikie, hiding his fear, winked at Leah and reached for the doorknob. To his surprise, the door slowly opened with hardly even a touch. It was as if another hand had opened the door to welcome them inside. Leah turned around to look towards her friends, hoping they would call off the dare, but she could neither see nor hear them. Holding her breath, she held onto Mikie's belt as he stepped inside.

In the semi-darkness, they could see three rooms on the first floor—a kitchen, parlour, and study. The skeleton remains of several small rodents were scattered across the kitchen floor and above the sink, a torn and frayed curtain blowing softly in the wind covered a broken window. In the hallway, they stopped at the bottom of the stairs and looked up. Mikie turned to Leah and let out a tense breath, winked again, took her hand, and hesitantly led the way up the dark staircase. The terms of the dare obligated them to explore every bedroom then stay inside the master bedroom—the room where the hanging was supposed to have taken place—until midnight.

The doors to two of the bedrooms were open, and they jumped as a bat flew from one bedroom to the other. Leah was now so frightened that she couldn't move, and she stood trembling behind Mikie. She watched him peer into the open doors of the two bedrooms then move further down the hallway to the last bedroom. Mikie put his ear to the closed door and listened. He beckoned Leah to come down but she couldn't move. But nothing had happened so far, which gave Mikie a false sense of bravado. He imagined himself a hero to everyone in the morning, which spurred him on to open the door and disappear inside.

No sooner was Mikie inside the room when the door slammed shut behind him. Leah waited through a long silence. Suddenly she heard a scream and a thump from inside the room. Leah forced herself over to the door, but she couldn't open it and pounding on it, she screamed for Mikie. There was no answer, only a deathly silence.

Leah stumbled down the stairs and ran outside to summon help from her hiding friends. When she told them what had happened to Mikie and begged them to go back inside with her, they ran away. Too terrified to go back by herself, she got on her bicycle and pedalled furiously home.

When she told her father what happened, he laughed and said, "Your friends were playing a joke on you."

"No, no," Leah said, "it wasn't that way at all."

She begged her father to go back with her, but he said, "In the morning."

By light of day and with her father in the lead, Leah once again climbed the stairs of the abandoned house. She pointed to the room that Mikie had entered, noticing that the door was now partly ajar. "In there, in there."

Her father shook his head and said, "I'll bet you a week's pay we'll find nothing but an empty room."

He pushed opened the door and went inside, where he immediately froze. There lying on the floor was the body of Mikie and lying under him was a mannequin.

Perhaps Mikie had bumped into the mannequin in the dark and, thinking he'd met a ghost, dropped dead of sheer fright. But was it really the mannequin that caused Mikie's death? Or was it something else?

The Haunted Privy

*D*riving through Nova Scotia's Cumberland County last summer, I saw several abandoned privies and it reminded me of a story I heard some time ago. Between gales of laughter, the storyteller had recounted a city woman's episode inside a haunted privy.

Elvira fled back to the house and raced upstairs to the guest bedroom she and her husband were occupying while on vacation. She shook him awake and rattled on in a panic about something very strange in the privy. When he got his senses back, he asked her what was so odd about the old privy. She told him that though she hadn't seen anyone, she'd had a strong feeling that someone was watching!

"Ridiculous," said the husband, "Last time I was in there, I didn't see or feel anything different."

Elvira took her husband by the hair, lifted his head off the pillow, and whispered hard against his ear, "I felt something and it was very close. I know something brushed by me."

The exasperated husband, now fully awake, tried to make sense of what his wife was blabbering about. "You said you didn't see anyone."

"That's right, I didn't."

"Well," her husband said, "if you didn't see anyone, then there was no one there, right?"

Between clenched teeth, Elvira said, "I'm telling you, there was."

"Well then," her husband calmly replied, "There's only one explanation, isn't there? The privy must be haunted." With that, he rolled over and went back to sleep.

With ten days remaining in their holiday, Elvira wondered how she was going to cope with nature's calls. One thing was for certain—no more privy for her.

During breakfast, Elvira's tactless husband told his brother and sister-in-law about Elvira's midnight adventure in the privy.

"Oh, is that old fart back again?" asked his brother, "He's been silent for so long we thought he'd crossed over for good."

Both Elvira and her husband looked at each other in shock while the brother told the story of Crapper John and his privy prison.

For a long time John's wife had suspected that her husband had more than a passing fancy for the maid, but she could never catch them. Until one day, that is, when the call of nature had her rushing to the privy. She was about to open the privy door when she heard heavy breathing coming from inside. She hurried to the barn and grabbed a milking stool to place below the small window. She climbed up, but nearly fell off when she saw what was going on.

She disappeared into the house, and returned loading a twelve gauge. Quietly she placed the shotgun against the door and readied herself. Crapper John opened the door to see if the coast was clear, and she fired both barrels. Before the good wife could re-load, however, the pretty young thing was off over hill and dale, never to be seen or heard from again. Crapper John's widow stepped over his body and dropped the shotgun down the crapper. She blamed it on the vanished maid and got away with murder.

"I've been told," said the brother on finishing the tale of Crapper John, "that ghosts are afraid of three things. First, other ghosts. Second, crossing the road. And third, the dark. So when you use the privy next, don't turn the light on."

To that end, the two brothers boarded the window and sealed off any cracks that allowed light to filter in. When the job was done, the brothers celebrated with a local brew, sitting over the appropriate openings. With a sudden heave, the platform they were sitting on was overturned!

Needless to say, Elvira, with a well-scrubbed husband in tow, was on the next train bound for the city.

Chapter Two

Roadside Spectres

The Ghost on the Lonely Road

*C*lyde Ehler drove the deserted back road through worsening weather—high wind and rain that came down in torrents. It was, as they say, a day for neither man nor beast. But there was someone else on the lonely stretch of road that day and Clyde Ehler was, unfortunately, in the wrong place at the wrong time.

Clyde was near Six Mile Brook in Pictou County when he saw the old woman walking along the road. He slowed down as he approached her, noting how old she looked and what peculiar clothes she wore. Straight out of the nineteenth century, with a shawl draped over her head. When Clyde stopped to ask if she needed help or a ride, she was nowhere to be seen. Worried that she may have somehow fallen under the truck, Clyde got out and looked everywhere. But she had simply vanished.

Driving away, Clyde passed a graveyard and felt a cold chill run through his body. Was she the ghost of some unhappy soul that died many years ago?

Clyde remembered how he'd smiled, hearing others tell stories of a ghost-woman on the road. Clyde Ehler isn't smiling anymore.

The Woman on the Road

*W*hat lies ahead? What's around the next turn in the road? We mere mortals can't know. Marilyn Matthews didn't know what was ahead when she and her mother were driving her young sister to Saint Anne's College in western Nova Scotia.

After saying their goodbyes, Marilyn and her mother decided to look for lodgings for the night rather than drive back to Halifax. Unfortunately it was the Labour Day weekend and there was not a room to be had in the area. Around 2:00 A.M. they became concerned that they wouldn't find a place to stay, and Marilyn's mother began to cry.

Nearing Smith's Cove, they were shocked to see an old woman appear suddenly in front of the car. She waved her arms in the air and told them to turn around and go back. Marilyn pleaded with her to move off the road, and tried to get her mother to drive on, but the old woman wouldn't budge from their path. She kept telling them to go back, ignoring Marilyn's pleas to move off the road. It was as if she didn't hear her. There was nothing to do but turn around and go back. They continued to drive until they saw another motel and, after waking the owner, they were given a room for the night.

It's been over 25 years since that terrible night and Marilyn Matthews wonders to this very day if the old woman on the road was flesh and bone...or a ghost.

Twinkie's Corner

Some place names are bland, even forgettable. Then there are the ones that slow you down and make you take notice. One name in particular is a sure attention-getter—Twinkie's Corner in Shag Harbour, Nova Scotia. A name like Twinkie certainly needs further investigation. What's behind such a name? Did something memorable or terrible happen?

According to a letter I received from Mrs. Edith Roth of Shag Harbour, the place got its name from an unfortunate event that ended a whole lifetime of unfortunate events.

Born in the mid-1850s, John "Twinkie" Nickerson spent all his miserable days trying to eke out a living for his family. He was so destitute at times that he was forced to feed his family from the entrails of animals he scrounged from neighbours. Twinkie's life never held much pleasure to begin with. But his misery was compounded when his wife died and his children grew up and moved out to live their own lives. Twinkie felt that life was no longer worth living, so he ended it by hanging himself in his shabby bedroom.

John "Twinkie" Nickerson was buried in an unmarked grave in a place that would come to be known as "Twinkie's Corner." There are those who believe that the spirit of a suicide victim can never rest and will return to haunt the living. Before the grave was filled in, a relative drove a wooden stake through the coffin in the belief that such an act would keep Twinkie's spirit from coming back from the dead.

I don't know of anyone who has actually seen Twinkie's ghost—but on foggy nights, Twinkie's Corner is avoided by those who know their Shag Harbour history.

The Ghost of Ghost Hollow

It seems that some ghosts have a sense of humour, and will go to any lengths to drive those who are still in this world nearly into the next.

There is a place on New Brunswick's Grand Manan Island known as Ghost Hollow where a little old spirit who wears a crazily tilted black hat scares the bejesus out of drivers who happen to be travelling over the road on dark and foggy nights.

This little tease of a ghost will suddenly come racing out of the woods and run alongside a car, grinning from ear to ear. He'll then pick up his speed and when he's a step or two ahead, throw himself in front of the car. The driver, a breath away from a heart attack, slams on the brakes and gets out to help the old man, but there's never anyone there. Baaaad ghost.

The wheelbarrow Ghost

While researching the Lady in Blue at Indian Harbour, a story that appeared in my first *Maritime Mysteries* book, I was told about another spirit. This one was about an old fisherman dressed in black oilskins who was seen in the community from time to time, pushing a wheelbarrow along Middle Point Road, perhaps headed for the harbour. Many have wondered who he was and where he came from, and were very curious to know the contents of the wheelbarrow. Those who have seen him have attempted to steal a glance at what he's pushing. But just as soon as someone tries to get a closer look, he's gone into the mist, if there is any. And when ghosts surround us, there usually is.

Chapter Three

Forerunners and Premonitions

A Gift, or a Curse

*T*here are people who have the gift of seeing into the future. Some don't call it a gift really, but a curse. They see things that we don't, and what they see most is the coming of death. This gift or curse is, I'm told, prevalent among Scottish descendants. I suppose that's why we hear more of these stories happening on Cape Breton Island than anywhere else. Here are a few hair-raisers from Dr. Helen Creighton's excellent book, *Bluenose Ghosts*. If it's not on your bookshelf, I recommend you include it.

There was a woman who lived in Mira who could see a funeral ahead of time, even before the person had been stricken. This woman would even know whose funeral it was. Sometimes when it happened, she would be walking along the road and be pushed to one side by the mourners following the hearse. The experience was always exhausting because not only could she feel the passing procession, but she would know the people in it.

Another story of insight involved a Mr. McNeil of Bras d'Or who was down by the shore one day when two young men came along looking for a boat. Mr. McNeil warned them they must not go out in a boat on this particular day.

"If you go," he told them, "one of you will not come back alive and the other will nearly drown."

The young men laughed at the old man, then got in the boat and rowed off. Sure enough, their boat capsized and one of the young men went under and was never found. The other surely would have drowned if he had not been rescued by the crew of a passing vessel. Just before he went down for the last time, his rescuers grabbed him by the hair on his head and lifted him to safety.

A tale from Marion Bridge was related by Alex Morrison, son of the local blacksmith. A boy named Neil McPherson was crossing the bridge with his mother when he looked over the side and said, "Come here, mother, and see the little boy lying on the bottom of the river."

She couldn't see anything and told her son to come along home.

It wasn't long after that little Sandy Munro drowned, but the story doesn't end there. About that time, people were seeing a light up the river near Grand Mira. There was a boat for sale but nobody would buy it because the light made them suspicious that it was a bad luck boat. Alex the blacksmith said, "I want it, light or no light," so he bought it.

Foul play was always suspected in the death of young Sandy. The night before Sandy died, the irons in the smithy were making a terrible racket. You could hear them in the forge and they seemed to be jumping around. Young Sandy and the blacksmith were friends and Sandy often did errands for him. Just before Sandy died, the blacksmith had asked him to take an axe across the bridge to a customer. Young Sandy was apparently doing just that when he met two other boys who were of bad character, the sons of a supposed witch. Someone reported seeing the boys tussling on the bridge, and some time later the body of young Sandy was found lying in the water as Neil McPherson had described to his mother.

They called on the blacksmith to get the body. The grappling irons he used to get the boy were the same ones that had jumped around in the forge the night before, and the boat he used to get Sandy was the one that had shown the strange looking light. After the body was discovered his mother had a strange dream, that the boy came to her and pointed to the blacksmith's axe as it stood at its place in the forge and said, "That's the axe that killed me."

When Sandy's body was laid out on the bridge of the boat Alex had bought, a lot of people from the village came to look at him. One was the boy who was supposed to have murdered him. There is a belief that if a murderer passes by or touches the person he murdered, blood will flow from the wound. As the suspected murderer walked by the body, blood flowed from the wound in Sandy's temple and stopped as soon as he passed. The thing was hushed up and the boys and their mother moved away. "But," Alex Morrison says, "That's the way it all happened."

The Wake

The young man was saddened by the death of his friend. The funeral parlour was dim and crowded, and he went into the wrong viewing room in confusion. The sight of the body lying in the coffin sent him reeling out into the night.

As soon as he got home he told his wife that he had seen himself being waked. With tears in her eyes, she suggested that he had witnessed a forerunner, a warning of a tragedy—perhaps his own death!

The next morning he kissed his wife goodbye and left for work. She stood in the doorway until her husband disappeared down the road, wondering if she'd ever see him alive again.

Late that afternoon the young man received an urgent call from his parents. An automobile accident had claimed the life of his brother—his identical twin!

The Point Wolf Forerunner

At a reading of my first book, *Maritime Mysteries*, in the Port Greville Age of Sail Museum, I met a man named Clayton Colpitts. Clayton was a 95-year-old gentleman who, before retiring, was a heavy equipment operator, an artist, and a poet. He is still writing poetry. Clayton Colpitts had a story to tell about messages from beyond.

The year was 1922 and the story occurred in Point Wolf, New Brunswick. Clayton was fifteen years old and, like most of the people of Point Wolf, worked at the local pulp mill. One of the mill workers was a young man of twenty by the name of Victor Cahill. Victor was a well-built man of some two hundred pounds who was very friendly to everyone. He especially liked Clayton Colpitts and his friends.

On the night in question, there was a dance at the local hall. Clayton and his friends were too young to attend so they decided to slip into a neighbor's orchard and steal some apples instead. They walked along a pond just below the pulp mill, commenting on how clear and calm the water was. "Like a mirror," one said.

No sooner had he said that, than a small ripple began to take shape, spreading outward and flashing all the colours of the rainbow. All the colours melted into an ominous dark red before vanishing completely. The boys had no idea what it was, and continued on to the apple orchard.

On the way back they stopped at the dance hall to watch the older people dancing. There was, as Clayton recalls, a lot of liquor being freely passed around. One of the revellers was a young black man from the United States by the name of Charles Brown, a cook aboard a schooner that had arrived in port only a few days before. One of the locals told Brown that Victor Cahill was making racist comments about him, so Brown sought out Cahill and told him what he had heard. The two eventually made peace, shook hands, and went back into the dance.

The peace didn't last long. The same man told Brown that Cahill was still making comments about his colour. Both men went outside to settle matters, and Clayton and the others stayed to watch. It was dark where the men stood and though no blows were exchanged, Clayton heard Victor saying, "Someone has vomited on my back..."

It wasn't vomit, but blood pouring from a stab wound. The back of Victor's white shirt began turning red, the same colour Clayton and his friends had seen on the water earlier that evening.

Victor Cahill died from his wounds. Charles Brown was convicted of murder and sentenced to twenty years in Dorchester penitentiary. And when Clayton Colpitts thinks about the ominous red colour of the water that night, he is certain he witnessed a forerunner of his good friend's death.

The Scotch Settlement Forerunner

*M*any Maritime stories have been lost because no one thought of putting them down on paper. By their very folkloric nature, such stories should be preserved for future generations.

Reverend Roger MacPhee of Hartsville, Prince Edward Island brought this story to my attention. Had his wife Kathie not wisely documented the story, it may have been, like many others, lost forever. The main character in this forerunner tale is Reverend Roger MacPhee's grandfather Reverend Donald Nickleson.

Reverend Nickleson was born at the turn of the century in Scotch Settlement, known today as Hartsville. Young Donald's grandparents, like most of the families in the settlement, were immigrants from Scotland and their spoken language was Gaelic. There were six children in the Nickleson family. Donald's father was a wandering soul who had mined for gold in Colorado and worked harvesting and logging in the camps of Northern Ontario. Donald's mother shouldered the responsibility of running the home and farm.

In his own words, this is what Reverend Nickleson told his children and grandchildren.

"I recall one warm July evening when a mysterious event occurred in our lives. I was ten at the time. My brother Murdock and I were milking the cows in the back field. When we returned to the house the sun was setting behind the hill. My mother and sister were standing on the porch and when she saw us she beckoned us to come over. 'What noise is that, do you think,' she asked.

"I listened and heard a strange squealing sound rather like iron rubbing against iron. We kept listening and could hear the noise as it moved along the road in the valley below our house, but it was too dark to see anything. When the noise came to our gate it stopped. We could hear voices but could see nothing. Our mother recognized one of the voices. 'That's Dan MacKay,' she said. Then the noise started up again and we could hear it moving away for more than half a mile.

"The following Sunday we saw Dan MacKay at church. When we asked him about it, he said he had been home all evening. It was all very strange and as the months passed we had forgotten about the incident. It remained a mystery until the following winter. On a bitterly cold morning, mother went outside for some kindling. She called us outside. 'Did you ever hear that noise before?' she asked.

We immediately recognized it as the same noise we heard on that summer evening. The light of day revealed the scene before us in the valley below. We could see a procession of horse-drawn sleighs winding slowly through the deep snow. As we found out later, the people were returning from the train station in North Wilshire where they had met the remains of an elderly woman who passed away in Boston. They were accompanying her body to the church in Kelly's Cross for burial. When the funeral procession got to our gate, who did we see coming from the opposite direction, but Dan MacKay himself, riding in his sleigh. The funeral procession stopped right at our gate and we heard them talking just as we had that summer before. Finally the funeral procession moved on. But now on this cold and frosty morning we had finally solved the mystery of the noise. It was caused by the high-pitch squeal the sleigh's runners made scraping over the packed snow. We never knew who the elderly lady from Boston was nor why we were witness to her forerunner of death."

Reverend Donald Nickleson passed away in 1998 at the age of 92.

Spectral Cats

While talking to Joyce Cook about growing up on Croucher's Island, Nova Scotia, I discovered that her late grandmother was a fortune teller and that Joyce herself had what some call ESP.

The day before her father died, Joyce's husband and children were at the local ballfield. Joyce was upstairs when she heard her husband's car come in the yard. She remembers distinctly hearing her husband's familiar footsteps come into the house, whixh Joyce thought was peculiar since the men in her family had only left an hour earlier for the ball game.

When she went downstairs, there was no one there nor was the car in the yard. Joyce realized it was a forerunner when her father died the next day. No one can explain to Joyce Cook why it was her husband and not her father in the forerunner manifestation.

Joyce told me that another message of impending doom invaded her home the day before her mother passed away. It wasn't a picture of a loved one or a calendar falling off the wall—she saw ghostly black cats roaming the house. When she was told her mother had died, the cats disappeared.

Mill Pond Forerunner

*T*hese stories are from the late Elsie Churchill Tolson's book *The Captain, the Colonel and Me*, which chronicles the history of Bedford, Nova Scotia, its people, and its ghosts! I've taken some liberties with these stories but have not embellished them to the degree that the facts are dramatically changed or distorted.

It was December 2, 1929, and as usual thirteen-year-old Gordon Lively of Millview was making the rounds of his paper route. Around noon of the same day, another young boy, sixteen-year-old James Wyatt, had found his Christmas present hidden in a closet—a pair of skates. Young James Wyatt just couldn't wait, so he slipped out of the house and headed for the pond by Moir's Mill. Another boy by the name of Dauphinee joined Gordon for an afternoon of skating. These are ordinary children doing ordinary things. But what happens next is out of the ordinary.

What was guiding or controlling Gordon Lively that day? Why did he arrive at the pond at the exact moment the lives of two boys where threatened? Ordinarily Gordon would have taken much longer delivering his papers because it was collection day. But for some unexplained reason, Gordon hurriedly dropped off the papers and headed for the pond, just in time to hear young Dauphinee calling out that James was drowning. Gordon, who was a boy scout, dropped his paper bag and ran out onto the ice to help James. But in his efforts to save young James Wyatt, he too drowned.

The night before, Gordon's sister Lillian had had a frightening dream of a white horse galloping towards her and rearing up to reveal a finger ring attached to its foreleg. That frightening nightmare stayed with Lillian all the next day and she could not shake off the feeling that something dreadful was going to happen.

"When they found my brother," said Lillian, "his arm was thrust up above the water—and on his finger was the ring we had given him!"

Rock of Ages

*A*re you still skeptical? Do you find it hard to believe that there could possibly be something to the forerunner phenomenon? Well then, perhaps this early-1900s tale will convince you otherwise. It involves several salmon fishermen from Grey Rapids, New Brunswick, who would cast their nets upon the waters every evening. Around midnight, they'd take an hour break and come ashore where they'd gather for a cup of hot tea and sandwiches at Dave Coughlan's general store.

Late one evening, while gathered on Dave's front lawn discussing this and that, the fishermen heard the hymn "Rock of Ages" being played on an organ. It was suggested that Becky Coughlan, Dave's sister-in-law, was practising her hymns for Sunday services. The next moment, however, the startled men saw a team of black horses and a hearse coming over the hill. The fishermen watched with their mouths agape as the hearse and team of horses lifted straight off the road and up into the night sky.

The next morning, word spread throughout the community that Becky had died in her sleep. Two days later the same fishermen observed a hearse with a team of six black horses carrying the remains of Becky Coughlan to the church. Inside the church, the fishermen once again looked at each other and nodded their heads as they listened to the first hymn being sung by the choir. It was "Rock of Ages."

I thank Lawrence and Elva Arbeau of Riverview, New Brunswick for this forerunner story.

Chapter Four

Mystery at Sea

Cheney's Ghost

When I inquired about the ghost of Cheney Island, the people of Grand Manan would shrug their shoulders and move on, mumbling something about rattling chains, screams, and splashing water. I was trying to investigate an intriguing ghost story that Richard Hire of Moncton told me while I was in the city promoting my first book. Back in the mid-seventies, Richard was a tax assessor. While searching land titles for the New Brunswick government, he heard snippets about a wandering ghost on and off Cheney Island.

Back in the mid-1800s, it was business as usual for many sea-captains who not only skirted the law, but put their very lives on the line for a quick buck.

During the building of the railroads in North America in the 1800s, immigration of Chinese labour was under strict government supervision. To enforce the law, British warships patrolled the coastal waters of the Maritimes. The penalty for smuggling these labourers was death by hanging.

There was a man by the name of Captain Cheney who was said to be involved in such unlawful activity. Perhaps these rumours merely began because he was a successful sea captain with a grand home on an island named after him. Or perhaps they were true. Regardless, one story tells us that a certain captain returning from the Orient had several Chinese illegals hidden below deck. When he spotted two British warships bearing down on his ship, he had the Chinese tied to the anchor chain and sent them to their death in the Bay of Fundy.

Two telephone workers were the first to see the ghost of Captain Cheney. It was mid-afternoon and the men were on Cheney Island checking lines and digging post holes when out of nowhere a strange-looking elderly man appeared before them. He was dressed in the sea captain's uniform of the day—the day being a nineteenth-century day.

"And what, may I ask, are you doing?" inquired the ghost of ol' Captain Cheney.

When the workers tried to explain, Captain Cheney's ghost told them they were trespassing and ordered them to leave. The employees were not aware at the time they were in the presence of a ghost. When they returned to Grand Manan, they told their supervisor about the stranger they had encountered on Cheney Island, and warned him that the power company would likely hear from the old man accusing them of trespassing. Their boss smiled and told them to forget it. The man they had spoken to was a ghost—the ghost of Captain Cheney who had been dead for over a hundred years.

There were other appearances by the ghost of old man Cheney. When summer residents arrived on Grand Manan and the other islands in the Bay of Fundy, their children reported that a strange-looking man in a uniform sometimes watched them swimming or playing along the beach. The stranger never attempted to speak to them. He would only watch from a distance.

And what about the unfortunate Orientals who were sent to a watery grave? When the waters of the bay are calm, some fishermen swear they hear the clanking of chains and the wailing of voices speaking in some foreign tongue. Is that what keeps the ghost of Captain Cheney ever bound to wander above ground? Ah, those Maritime Mysteries of the sea!

The Rowing Ghost

Now to the mysterious sound of the rowing ghost. On foggy nights you can hear his oars splashing in the water. Some people have reported seeing an outline of a man's hunched-over shoulders slowly rowing back and forth. Other times people have reported a boat being hauled up on shore—but when they go down to investigate, no one is there.

Nobody can explain what may have happened to sentence this ghost to his endless rowing, and perhaps his story will never be told.

Shiver Me Timbers

Even when you think you've heard it all, you haven't. Here's a whale of a Nova Scotia tale that'll rattle your bones.

The old fisherman lifted his head and sniffed the salt air that came rolling in from the ocean, taking his good old time telling me this story. With those deep-set blue eyes of his, dimmed by too many suns, he finally turned his weather-beaten face to me and began his tall tale.

"I was alone at the time. The sun was just up and I was repairing my lobster traps just like I'm doin' now when I caught sight of him— it. He was coming out of the water, about a hundred yards off. There was not a stitch of skin on 'im. Just all bones. I watched him come ashore, shake off the seaweed, and with purpose in mind rattle my way. Well, sir, I must tell you I was some scared. I mean, a ghost is bad enough—but a skeleton ghost! When he saw me, I'm sure I scared the life out of him because his jaw dropped wide open. He just stood there glaring at me. Then he cocked his bony head to one side, looked me straight in the eye with those empty sockets of his, and then I swear he grinned from ear to ear and went straight by me, heading up the road towards town.

"Funny thing, though, I think he knew me. Of course, I couldn't really have recognized him. Still, he did look somewhat familiar. Something about the way he walked."

When I asked the old fisherman if he had formed an opinion as to what had happened to the ghost, he thought about it for awhile and then nodding, said, "He could have been one of us—a local fisherman, I mean. Or maybe a weekend sailor who fell overboard and drowned."

"And the skeleton?" I asked.

Again he shook his old head, "I donno, maybe the sea lice and fish cleaned him right down to the bone. It don't matter, though—he probably don't even know he's a skeleton ghost."

"So," I said, "that's it?"

"Not quite," he said, "not quite. Some time later I see him, the skeleton that is, coming back down the shore road. This you won't believe. That old bag-o-bones waved a bony arm at me and went right back into the sea, grinning from ear to ear!"

"What was he doing up town?" I asked.

"Seeing the Misses, I s'pose," the old fisherman replied. He, too, was grinning from ear to ear.

Now I've heard it all.

The Ghost of Double Alex

In 1964 John Fairservice and his family set off on the three-and-a-half-mile journey from Halifax to outer Sambro Island where John would live and work as lighthouse keeper for the next 24 years.

Perhaps one named Alex Alexander was waiting on that desolate shore. Known as Double Alex, he was not the retiring keeper of the light nor was he part of a welcoming committee. No, Double Alex was, and is, a nineteenth-century ghost.

How did Double Alex become a ghost? It was the demon rum, and a good time in some of the off-limit Halifax houses that did him in. There are multiple versions of how Double Alex ended up a spirit. I include the more popular one here.

Back in the early 1800s, British warships approaching Halifax Harbour were forced to use cannon fire to remind the lighthouse keeper that there wasn't sufficient light to guide their ships into safe waters. The problem was not the keeper, but poor illumination. To correct the situation, a contingent of light artillerymen were stationed on Sambro in 1833, and the army installed signal and fog cannons to guide the ships home.

One of the artillerymen assigned to the island at the time was quartermaster sergeant Alex Alexander, who frequently went into Halifax to purchase supplies. Alex had a problem with liquor, though, and he weakened on one such trip to Halifax. Ol' devil rum won the day. Alex went on a drinking and spending spree for an entire week and when it was over, he had spent every last cent he had been given to buy supplies.

When the military caught up with Alex, he was arrested and returned to Sambro to face charges. While in prison and suffering from the "dts," Double Alex begged for the "hair of the dog" cure, but the Colonel wouldn't allow Alex to have a single drop. That refusal was the proverbial straw that drove Alex to a self-made gallows. But before the last breath left his body, he was discovered and cut down by the guards.

It was suggested, as was the custom of the day, that Alex should be bled to start his heart pumping again, but that was against military rules. The colonel refused, and Double Alex drew his last breath and died. There are no documents revealing where his body is buried but there is evidence that his restless spirit is haunting Sambro Island.

It never crossed the minds of John Fairservice and his family that their new home might be haunted by a nineteenth-century ghost. Until one foggy morning when John stepped out of the lighthouse into an early morning fog, that is. Walking toward his home, he heard someone behind him. The fog was so thick that he couldn't see his hand in front of him, or anything behind. He listened for a long time but did not hear or see anything, so he cautiously continued walking. No sooner did he take a step when he heard the noise again. He stopped, turned, looked into the fog, and listened, but could see nothing. That was when he noticed coins from his pocket rolling along the walkway in front of him. John had a hole in one of his pockets, so he told himself the dropped coins had caused the mysterious noise. Nearly convinced himself, too.

But one day a short time later, John was alone in the house when he heard a knock on the door. He opened the door, only to find that there was no one there. That night, his brother-in-law died. As far as John is concerned, the knock was a forerunner.

John Fairservice has never actually seen the ghost of Double Alex, but he has seen many wispy black shapes sweeping over the island. John recalls one time when he and his assistant, returning to the island, saw a man standing on the shore. He seemed to be waiting for them. As soon as they docked they looked for the stranger, but he was nowhere to be found.

Is Double Alex the only ghost on Sambro Island? Perhaps not.

John says that during violent storms you can hear above the crashing waves the ghostly cries of people shipwrecked in the past. Perhaps they're the black shapes that haunt Sambro light.

Possessed

*T*he place where this frightful tale of possession happened is lost in folklore, and usually depends on who is telling the story. The time period of the incident is the mid-1920s.

While taking pictures of fishing boats, a young photographer nearly passed out when he saw a shadowy black form hovering over the tied-up boats. He watched as it swooped down, and the young man thought whatever it was either entered a certain fisherman's body, or vanished. He was also aware that for a brief moment it became very cold.

The young man watched as the fisherman guided his small craft the *Holly* through the channel and out to sea. He remained on the wharf watching until the boat was but a dot on the horizon. Would he be laughed at if he told the other fisherman what he saw? He decided to keep it to himself for the time being.

Next morning, he overheard two men discussing the mysterious disappearance of their friend and his boat. The photographer wondered if the lost fisherman was the same man whose body he believed may have been entered by an evil spirit. He drove directly to the wharf where he learned that a full-scale search for the lost fisherman was underway.

"Yes," they told him, "the name of the boat was the *Holly*."

It was sundown when the search boats came into port. Two men lifted the drowned fisherman into the waiting arms of the men on the wharf. A piece of canvas was placed over the body.

The fishermen stood around talking while they waited for the police to arrive. The photographer's attention was drawn by a slight movement to the body of the fisherman, as if a small animal such as a cat were crawling from under a blanket. But what slithered out from under the canvas was the same dark form, pausing a moment before flying off into the night.

Storm clouds were forming in the western sky when the young photographer started back to the city. A draught of cold air suddenly sent a chill through his body. He closed the windows and turned up the heat. But the temperature inside the car kept dropping.

The Saladin Murders

I can't promise the likes of a Captain Kidd or Long John Silver in this seafaring tale, but I can offer a voyage of high adventure complete with mutiny and murder. The story reads like a Hollywood script but is, in actual truth, documented fact.

The sounds of saws and hammers echoed across the Halifax South Commons as carpenters constructed a gallows for a public hanging. It was July 30, 1844, a warm and bright Saturday morning, when four young men mounted the steps of the scaffolding to be hanged. But before the trapdoors drop, let's examine the dastardly deeds that brought them to the ends of their ropes.

In February of that year, the British barque *Saladin* was prepared to set sail from the port of Valparaiso to London with a rich cargo of guano, silver, gold, and hard currency. Before leaving, four of the *Saladin*'s crew jumped ship, forcing the skipper to hire four unsavoury types.

These new deck hands would play a major role in the drama, but the high sea crime was born in the black and murderous heart of George Fielding of England. Fielding was born in Jersey, but was raised in the Gaspé where his father was a soldier for many years.

In October of 1843, Captain George Fielding, along with his crew and fourteen-year-old son, set sail from Liverpool, England for Buenos Aires in the barque *Vitula*. Finding freight at a premium in Buenos Aires, Fielding sailed to Valparaiso where the situation was no better. He was determined not to return to England with an empty ship, so he decided to smuggle a cargo of guano—a rich fertilizer—out of the country. But his scheme was discovered by the Peruvian government and fifty soldiers were sent to take over the *Vitula* and arrest him. Whether a brave man or a fool, Fielding would not give up without a fight. A gun battle broke out and Fielding was wounded. He was arrested and the *Vitula* and her cargo were confiscated by the government to be sold.

After his release from hospital, Fielding was given the freedom of the port of Callao. He proposed a plan to sneak aboard the *Vitula* and slip out of port. His scheme, however, was uncovered and he was again arrested, but this time he ended up in prison.

With the help of his son, Fielding escaped and hitched a ride aboard a freighter to the port of Valparaiso. Fielding was now a skipper without a ship, broke and stranded in a foreign land. His attempt to gain free passage to England was fruitless, as the captains of these vessels were aware of Fielding's exploits and wanted nothing to do with him. Finally, Captain Sandy MacKenzie of the *Saladin* agreed to give Fielding and his son free passage back to England.

The *Saladin* was a magnificent barque of 550 tons, with a bronze figurehead of a turbaned Turkish male on its bowsprit. For anyone with larceny in his heart, *Saladin's* cargo was a temptation—a ticket to riches. The possibility didn't go unnoticed by Captain Fielding.

When the *Saladin* set sail from Valparaiso on February 8, 1844, she had a crew of 14 and two passengers—Fielding and his son. Sandy MacKenzie was a no-nonsense skipper who bullied his crew to the point of mutiny. It became clear to MacKenzie from the outset that he had made a mistake in inviting Fielding aboard his ship. Their arguments over seamanship and the treatment of the men escalated to the point that Fielding was no longer welcome at MacKenzie's dinner table.

Fielding set himself on a course of destruction that would go down in the history of sail as one of the most heinous acts ever committed on the high seas. He set his plan in motion by turning the men against their captain, encouraging unrest to the point of mutiny. His plan was simple—lure Captain MacKenzie up on deck during the night and kill him, along with those who sided with him. When the deed was done, set a course for the Gaspé or Newfoundland where they would share the bounty and disappear into foreign lands. In truth, however, Fielding had no intention of sharing anything with anyone.

Under cover of darkness, the murders of the captain and those loyal to him were carried out with systematic brutality. All the guns were locked in MacKenzie's cabin, so Fielding and his mutineers used axes and hammers instead. They began with the first mate, plying an axe to his skull and throwing him, wounded but still alive, overboard.

A cry of "man overboard!" brought the sleepy captain on deck. As soon as he appeared above the companionway hatch, he was struck on the head with a glancing blow. MacKenzie fought, tackling his assailant, but the others held him down while Fielding crushed his skull. Perhaps caught up in the moment, Fielding's son screamed, "Give it to him!"

Before he was hurled into the sea, Captain MacKenzie's last words were, "Oh, Captain Fielding!"

Before the night was over, four more innocent souls followed the captain and first mate into the bloody waters.

By morning light, the deck of the *Saladin* was awash in blood, and the four deck hands—the youngest 19 and the oldest only 23—repented somewhat. They realized what they had done and pledged they would kill no more. They refused Fielding's orders to murder the two remaining members—the cabin boy John Galloway and William Carr, the cook—who had been asleep below deck when the murders took place. When called on deck and informed of the evening's events, Carr pleaded for his life, but not Galloway. His only regret was not having a hand in Captain MacKenzie's death.

Taking charge, Fielding set a course away from England to Newfoundland and the Gaspé. Being untrustworthy himself, he had little faith in the loyalties of the men under him. To control a volatile situation that could explode at any given moment, Fielding took every precaution. He kept the liquor locked in MacKenzie's cabin. Everyone agreed that the weapons should be thrown overboard, including the axes and hammers used in the murders.

On Sunday morning, Fielding called the men together. They placed their hands on Fielding's bible and swore their loyalty to each other. However, Fielding lied about getting rid of all the guns. He had two pistols hidden, just in case.

The crew didn't trust him, and rightfully so. They spoke among themselves about what he might really be up to. It came to a head when they found the two guns Fielding said he had thrown overboard. When they confronted him, he denied all knowledge of the hidden weapons. A fight broke out and Fielding was overpowered. The crew bound and gagged him, along with his son, and locked them in separate cabins until a course of action could be decided on. No one slept that night, in fear that Fielding would get free and murder them while they slept.

In the morning, the men agreed that if they were to live, Fielding and his son had to die. They demanded that Carr and Galloway, whose lives had been spared, carry out the murders. Galloway refused, but Carr, along with one of the original mutineers, dragged Fielding to the rail and threw him overboard. Fielding's fourteen-year-old son, kicking and screaming, joined his father in death.

The mutineers made Galloway the navigator. The plan was to scuttle the ship, and take the money and run. But liquor and time got in the way. They waited too long. As the "Ballad of the *Saladin*" goes:

We mostly kept her into the wind
For we could do no more

On the morning of May 22, with all her sails set, *Saladin* drove hard on an island at the mouth of Country Harbour, known today as Saladin Point. The news of the beached ship spread quickly. Captain

Cunningham of the schooner *Billow* came alongside, but high winds and a heavy sea made it almost impossible to board her. One of *Saladin*'s crew begged Cunningham to come aboard and take over, insisting that they were too liquored-up to save her. The crew hauled Cunningham, by a rope tied to his waist, over the turbulent water to the deck of the stranded vessel. Once on board, Captain Cunningham directed the men to help him cut away the sheets and halyards to keep her stable. The crew told him that the ship was the *Saladin* out of Newcastle, England, in the care of Captain Sandy MacKenzie, who had become ill and died at sea. The ship's first mate and other crew members, they insisted, were washed overboard during a violent storm. The last log entry was made on April 14.

After spending 36 hours aboard the *Saladin*, Captain Cunningham made his report to the local magistrate in Country Harbour. He reported that the six young sailors had been somewhat confused and plainly in a drunken stupor. He found the captain's quarters in disarray with papers strewn over the floor, and an open chest brimming with money. *Saladin*'s manifest showed she carried 70 tons of copper; 13 bars of silver, each weighing 150 pounds; and a large quantity of spice valued at $9,000. The vessel had rolled over on her starboard side and the valuable cargo of guano had been washed away.

Cunningham sailed to Halifax and notified the admiralty of the situation. H.M.S. *Fair Rosamond* was dispatched to Country Harbour to put the men in chains and bring them back to Halifax to stand trial. The money, valued at 18,000 pounds, was deposited in a vault at the Bank of Nova Scotia for the ship's owners.

Sitting in the cells of the old penitentiary on the arm, Carr and Galloway sent for their lawyers and confessed to their involvement in the murders. Carr's confession concluded with this comment: "I make this disclosure because I cannot die with such a burden on my mind and I am perfectly ready to abide by the law of the country." Galloway ended his written confession by concluding: "I make this declaration because I fear to die without disclosing the truth. No man knows how soon I may die."

Carr and Galloway also implicated the other four men—George Jones of Ireland; William Trevaskiss, also known as Johnson, of the United States; John Hazelton of northern Ireland; and Charles Anderson of Sweden. The trial was quick. All four were found guilty and sentenced to be hanged. William Carr and John Galloway were also tried, but were acquitted. The jurors believed that they were forced to murder Fielding and his son under the threat of death.

The hanging of the four men became a public spectacle. A company of foot soldiers formed a circle around the scaffold to keep the good citizens at bay. Just before 10:00 A.M. the men came down Tower Road in prison wagons, accompanied on either side by marching guards with fixed bayonets.

The four mounted the gallows steps and took their places over the trapdoors. Jones kissed his fellow murderers goodbye and spoke briefly to the crowd. He told them that he was sorry for what he had done and expressed hope that God would forgive him. The others remained silent. Three clergymen—Roman Catholic and Anglican—knelt in prayer as a hush came over the crowd. The signal was given and the executioner pulled the rope, sending the young men into eternity.

Hazelton and Jones were buried in the Catholic cemetery on South Park Street. Trevaskiss and Anderson were buried in pauper's graves. It is said that one night a young Halifax doctor, in need of a cadaver, dug up Anderson's body. It was reported that his skull was on display in the provincial museum for a time.

Of the fourteen who sailed on the *Saladin*, only two remained alive—Carr and Galloway. Carr settled in Digby County where he lived to an old age. Galloway disappeared for good.

Footnote: In time, Saladin *was taken apart by wind, tide, and man. Her windows were built into a carpentry shop in Country Harbour. A plaster cast of the figurehead sits in the Maritime*

Museum of the Atlantic in Halifax. A Frederick W. Bezanson of Chicago, who had a Country Harbour connection, donated to the museum a Bible owned by Captain MacKenzie, as well as a starboard lamp. Captain George Fielding's trunk is to this day in the Yarmouth County Museum where this writer opened it. But like Fielding's dreams, it was empty.

The Money Pit

And the Maritime Mystery of all mysteries? Perhaps the money pit on Oak Island. If there's buried treasure anywhere, it has to be there. But who buried it? Was the booty squirrelled away by those old rascals of the sea, captains Kidd, Morgan, or Blackbeard? Or is it the biggest hoax of all time? We are no closer today to solving the Oak Island Mystery than when the first treasure seekers stepped on the island in the late 1700s.

Oak Island is one of 365 islands located in Mahone Bay off Nova Scotia's south shore. Some old salts claim the island is haunted and that seven people will die before it relinquishes its treasure. So far, six people have died while searching for the elusive booty.

So, how do we go about unravelling this two-centuries-old mystery? Folklore has it that it all started back in the early 1700s when three young men stumbled upon a depression in the earth. After exhaustive and extensive digging they found a perplexing network of tunnels and layers, but they came up empty-handed. After that first attempt, there was no stopping the rumours of a king's ransom buried on the island.

Who came ashore to dig the intricate series of shafts and bury the legendary treasure? According to engineers, the layers upon layers of architecture are nothing less than genius. Since the first rumour of buried treasure spread across the world, a lot of money, heavy equipment, and muscle have been used to no avail—the stash was superbly concealed. But dreams of finding the money pit still haunt the minds of more adventurous souls.

Perhaps the phantom pirate's gold will never be found. Perhaps the ocean washed it out to sea long ago.

A hoax? A mystery, certainly. And one that the Nova Scotia tourist industry folk hope will never be solved. It would be bad for business.

The Hole-In-The-Wall Pirates

There's a small village on Grand Manan Island known as Northhead which is home to a fascinating tale of three fishermen who had an identical dream of buried treasure. After comparing their visions, there was nothing left to do but gather up their picks and shovels and start digging at a spot some fifty feet from the high cliffs overlooking the Bay of Fundy.

As soon as the first spade was driven into the ground they heard the sound of rattling chains. Out of the mist rose a transparent ghost ship and on the bow stood a pirate swinging a sword over his head. The fishermen dropped their tools and fled in terror.

Basil Small is the owner and operator of a hiking park and campground. He told me how his father later found the spot. The tools were still where the fishermen had dropped them. He once showed Basil where the spade made a mark in the ground. Basil's father never did explain why he didn't look for the treasure. Perhaps he knew the ghosts were guarding their loot.

When Basil began operating the hiking and camping business he hired a psychic to find out where the treasure was buried, if it existed at all. He led her along the path but the psychic stopped suddenly. In a sort of trance, she led Basil to a place where she said a body was buried. Describing a vision that flashed before her eyes, she told him, "I see a man of the cloth wearing a flowing black robe coming toward us. He is followed by two sailors carrying a body. Now the sailors are digging a grave where we stand."

When the vision passed, Basil led her to where the three fishermen had once dug for the pirate's treasure. The psychic, with her eyes closed, shook her head and said, "There is no buried treasure here, or anywhere else on your land."

Really? Then what about the dream and the ghost ship?

And then there's the presence of a mysterious landmark nearby— the rock formation known as the Hole-In-The-Wall. Some say it's the portal where the spirits enter and leave our world.

Coincidence? Perhaps. Or perhaps Basil only tells this story to keep treasure-seekers off his property....

The Curse of the Mary Celeste

In my mind's eye, I'm standing on the shore at Spencer's Island where I see a young Joshua Dewis, builder of wooden ships, honing his craft. I close my eyes and listen beyond the Minas Channel surf to the ghostly sounds of carpenters, riggers, caulkers, and sawyers building Joshua's dream.

But that time is long past. The only remnants exist in memory, and in descendants like Isaac and Jacob Spicer who, in partnership with Joshua Dewis, supplied the lumber that became the island's first vessel—the *Amazon*. The name would later be changed to the *Mary Celeste*, that infamous hoodoo ship, that bad luck vessel.

What caused Dewis' first vessel to become a hoodoo vessel? Was she cursed by one of the workmen after a falling-out with Dewis? Was she bewitched by some evil spirit?

Much has been written about the disappearance of the *Mary Celeste* and her crew. In my search for the true story, I contacted Stanley T. Spicer, a direct descendant of Isaac and Jacob Spicer. Stan has written extensively on every vessel that was built on Spencer's Island, and in particular the *Mary Celeste*. I'm indebted to Stan for his generosity.

The story begins with Joshua Dewis of West Advocate, who needed an ideal location and accessible timber to build his dream vessels. He found both on Spencer's Island. Money, however, was a problem for young Dewis, so he met and struck a deal with brothers Isaac and Jacob Spicer—shares in the vessel for timber from their land. He made a similar arrangement with ship suppliers in Windsor, Nova Scotia, and in 1860 the keel of the brigantine *Amazon* was laid. In the following year the vessel was launched, beginning one of the most amazing Maritime Mysteries of the sea.

Jacob Spicer's son George began his seafaring career at the age of twelve, and when the Amazon was launched, fifteen-year-old George signed on.

During the *Amazon*'s maiden voyage, tragedy struck. While sailing up the Bay of Fundy to Five Islands to take on a cargo of lumber for England, recently-married Captain Robert MacLellan from Economy, Nova Scotia was stricken with pneumonia. He was forced to remain in his cabin while the Amazon was being loaded. Though he was determined to sail the *Amazon* on her maiden voyage to England, his condition worsened and the first mate turned the vessel back to Spencer's Island. Captain MacLellan died a few hours later in the home of young George Spicer.

The next morning the crew of the *Amazon* wrapped the body of Captain MacLellan in a blanket and set sail for his home in Economy. As the boat came into view, the new bride of the dead captain, anxious at the ship's hasty return, ran down to embrace her husband. George Spicer began his sea career as a cabin boy on the *Amazon* and before his seafaring career ended, he was the master of several vessels. Until his dying day, George Spicer never forgot that tragic moment when they brought the body of Captain MacLellan home to his young widow.

In the late 1860s, the *Amazon* went aground off Glace Bay, Cape Breton, during a gale. Her damage was major and following salvage, the *Amazon* changed ownership several times, ending up under American registration in 1868 with a new name, *Mary Celeste*.

On November 7, 1872, the *Mary Celeste* cleared New York harbour for Genoa, Italy, with a cargo of 1701 barrels of alcohol. On the bridge was 37-year-old Captain Benjamin Briggs out of Marion, Maine, accompanied by his wife Sarah and their two-year-old daughter Sophia. Including the crew, the ten people on board had no idea what lay in store for them.

On November 15, Captain David Reed Morehouse and the brigantine *Dei Gratia* from Bear River, Nova Scotia, left Hoboken, New Jersey for Gibraltar. The *Dei Gratia* encountered severe storms until November 24 and it is assumed that the *Mary Celeste* also fought the same weather conditions.

On the morning of December 4, midway between Portugal and the Azores, the *Dei Gratia* sighted a vessel off her port bow. The vessel was under short canvas and heading in a westerly direction, almost opposite to the *Dei Gratia* on her course southeast by east. The sea was running high but the weather was starting to moderate. The *Dei Gratia* changed course and hailed her, but there was no reply. Captain Morehouse sent his first mate Oliver Deveau with two seamen in a small boat to board what appeared to be an abandoned vessel.

It was the *Mary Celeste* of New York, and when the boarding party climbed up on her deck there was not a living soul to be found. The foresail and the upper foretopsail had been blown off the vessel but three sails were still set. The main staysail had been hauled down and was lying loose on the foreward house. All the other sails were furled. Some of the running rigging had been carried away, and sheets and braces hung loose over the side. The *Mary Celeste* carried only one life-boat, usually lashed on the main hatch, but it was gone. The binnacle (box) had been knocked down and the compass smashed. The cargo was in good shape with no evidence of shifting, fire, or explosion.

With salvage rights uppermost on their minds, Captain Morehouse allowed the first mate and two seamen to sail the *Mary Celeste* into Gibraltar. A vice-admiralty court was convened to hear the salvage claim of the *Dei Gratia*, and to investigate the disappearance of the captain, his family, and the ship's crew. During the hearing, Deveau and other members of the *Dei Gratia* testified that they could offer no explanation as to why the *Mary Celeste* had been abandoned.

The Queen's proctor and attorney general of Gibraltar Frederick Solly Flood ordered a survey of the *Mary Celeste*. When he was not satisfied with the results of the survey, Flood came up with his own theory. He suggested that the crew had gotten into the rum and murdered the captain and his family, as well as the first mate, in a drunken rage before fleeing in the ship's lifeboat. He went so far as to implicate Captain James H. Winchester, the owner of the *Mary Celeste*, as the mastermind behind the murders. Winchester hurried to Gibraltar to protect his interests, but fled back to the States when he found out Flood might arrest him. Flood's insistence on foul play was totally insubstantiated by the known facts but had the effect of prolonging the hearing and, perhaps due to the suspicions raised, resulted in the crew of the *Dei Gratia* receiving the relatively small award of about $8,300. Impartial authorities later estimated this to be roughly one-third of the amount that should have been granted, even before the costs of the inquiry were deducted.

The *Mary Celeste* was finally released and ended her sailing days when she drove ashore on the reef of the Rochelais off Haiti.

So what happened to the people aboard the *Mary Celeste*? Many theories have been advanced down through the years, ranging from murder for salvage, to a giant octopus that raised its tentacles out of the water and sucked every living soul off the ship.

But the more acceptable theory is the one advanced by Dr. Oliver W. Cobb of New Bedford, Massachussetts, an expert in such matters. Dr. Cobb said the *Mary Celeste* carried a dangerous cargo of alcohol which was loaded in cold water. When the vessel arrived in warmer temperatures the alcohol would naturally expand, perhaps causing leakage. One can picture what might have happened, and perhaps it went something like this:

On the morning of November 25, sometime after eight, Captain Briggs decided to take advantage of the more favourable weather to ventilate the hold. He ordered his crew to remove the forehatch, resulting in an uprush of vapour followed by ominous rumblings from below. The leakage amounted to nine barrels of alcohol and, fearing an explosion, Briggs gave orders to launch the lifeboat. He directed the crew to tether the boat with a long towline so that contact could be maintained with the ship while they waited to see if the cargo would explode. The crew started to get the rope from the lazarette and then decided that it was easier to use the main peak halyard. It was only a minute's work to pull it through the masthead and gall blocks, offering a line some three hundred feet in length.

The heavily-loaded small boat was being towed along by the *Mary Celeste* when a sudden and violent squall came up, causing the ship to spurt ahead, parting the towline or chafing the line where it came around a stanchion. It was a deadly day to be set adrift, as gale force winds and heavy rains were recorded in that region of the Azores.

Meanwhile, the *Mary Celeste* kept sailing on an unsteady course and in her lonely wanderings she sailed between five and six hundred miles.

We can imagine the scenario, but no one really knows what happened to the people on board the *Mary Celeste*. Oliver Deveau of the *Dei Gratia* said in his testimony, "Here was a vessel fully provisioned with food and water; with hull, masts, spars, and standing rigging in good shape; with only normal leakage; and, with the exception of two sails blown away, fit to go around the world."

When all is said and done, however, and as Stanley Spicer wrote in his book *The Saga of the Mary Celeste*, "the truth of what happened lies with the sea itself and the bones of the old vessel on the reef of the Rochelais."

Chapter Five

Restless Spirits and Unfinished Business

The Ghost in the Confessional

*T*he priest looked at his watch. It was getting late. No more sinners today, he thought. He was about to leave the confessional when he heard the door slowly open. He could see the outline of a person and heard a pitiful moan from whomever it was that knelt down.

In that semi-darkness, the priest could not make out the face pressed against the screen. After he blessed the confessor, he said, as he had spoken hundreds of times before, "Yes, my son, you have sins to confess?"

There was a long silence before the person began to speak. "Father, forgive me, but I am in great distress. Many years ago a man was murdered and I knew who the murderer was but said nothing. My conscience is heavy and if I'm to find peace, I must tell what I know. The murderer was Herman Somerville and his victim was Peter Castlemier who had a dagger plunged through his heart."

The priest waited but there was no more. When he got up and went around to the other side of the confessional the door was open and the speaker had disappeared.

The good father hurried back to the glebe house and told the other priests what had happened. An old priest sitting next to the fireplace put down his book and said, "There is only one person who would know who killed Peter Castlemier and that would be his murderer. You heard the confession of Herman Somerville himself."

The young priest, with a puzzled look on his face, didn't need to ask for an explanation. The old priest went on. "I arrived at the Castlemier home just minutes after the murder, on my way to visit Castlemier's gravely ill mother. I had just entered the front hall when I heard someone running and the back door closing. There, lying in a pool of blood in the hallway, was Peter Castlemier. Only the police and I knew the type of weapon that killed Castlemier. And, oh yes, one other person knew—the murderer."

The young priest was speechless. Herman Somerville had died years ago!

The Rope

I felt a tap on my shoulder one Sunday morning while in church and heard my fellow churchgoer whisper, "Got a good one for you, Bill. This is a Cape Breton ghost story. It's about a guy who borrowed a rope but never gave it back. It happened up north."

It seems a ghost was creating quite a disturbance in the village, roaming up and down the road and scaring a lot of people. He scared everyone except one man who said, "Enough is enough. Next time he appears, I'll confront him. Find out what he wants."

The brave villager waited one night until the ghost appeared and said, "In the name of all that's holy, what do you want?"

Well that stopped the ghost in his tracks all right. "I borrowed a rope from my neighbour to take my cow into a pasture, but before I could give it back, I died. The rope is still hanging in my barn. You give it back and I'll never bother anyone again."

Sure enough, the rope was where the ghost had said, and the villager gave it back to its owner. In turn, the ghost kept his word. He was never seen again.

Footnote: My friend in the back pew is a reader of Cape Breton folklore. He got the story out of Ronald Caplan's Cape Breton Book of the Night. *The story of the man who had borrowed a rope was an Amelia Cook yarn.*

Don't Touch

Step softly when visiting a cemetery. Speak in whispers and disturb nothing. And a stern warning for gravediggers. You'd be wise to listen to the old folk who will tell you to leave em' lay, and woe betide those who do not listen. Unfortunately, two young diggers did not heed the warning and had to pay the price.

While producing a story for ATV's "Maritime Mysteries," my camera crew and I spent some time on location in a cemetery down along the Eastern Shore. While the TV crew were setting up the lights and cameras, a tall elderly gentleman suddenly appeared out of nowhere and asked what we were doing. When I told him we were producing a ghost story, he told me to be very careful not to disturb anything, especially those who were in eternal sleep. To make his point, he told me why we should be careful. It's a story I have heard many times and in just as many variations.

"One time, my friend Henry and I were digging a grave and we dug up some old bones. I brought home a piece, and Harry took some pieces home too. In the morning when I looked out my bedroom window, I saw a woman going past the house. She was a tall woman in a long black coat. It was my intention to ask her to come in but when I went to the door to call her, she disappeared. I told Henry about it and he said she had walked past his house, too. We got talking about her and the more we thought about it, the more we didn't like it. We decided the bones might have had something to do with it, and agreed that we had better throw them away. We wondered if they might have belonged to a woman peddler who mysteriously disappeared years ago. After we put the bones back, we never saw the woman again."

When the stranger ended his graveside story, I thanked him and also assured him we would indeed be careful. He walked further into the graveyard and I watched until he disappeared into the trees. To this day, when I drive past that graveyard I don't think as much about the story as I do about the stranger I met and who he may have been. Perhaps he was one of those in eternal sleep? I wonder.

"You're Me," said the Ghost

While finishing last minute Christmas shopping, I had stopped for a burger at the food court when I was approached by an out-of-breath mother and her twelve-year-old daughter. The girl was fidgety and kept looking over her shoulder, as if expecting someone, or something. The mother exclaimed, "No names, please! Agreed?"

I invited them to sit down and join me, and the mother told her daughter, "Okay, tell him. You'll feel better."

For the first time, the young girl looked into my eyes as if she might find the answer to whatever was bothering her. By the look of her nails, bitten nearly to the quick, I knew she had a problem. Her voice quavered some as she told me about her two-hundred-year-old midnight visitor.

"It started when I was seven. One night I was awakened by someone nudging me on the shoulder. The room was dark and I thought it was my mother, but when I reached to turn on the light, a cold hand stopped me. I could see a dark outline and thought it was my brother trying to scare me. But then, whatever it was spoke. I knew it was not alive, I knew it was a ghost."

She paused, took a sip of her Coke and stared off into some other place. She told me that a spill of light from the moon was enough for her to see a hunched figure bending over her. "I was too scared to scream and too weak to get out of bed. The ghost said, 'You are me. You are my reincarnation, for it is you who must help me!' Then it disappeared. I jumped out of bed and ran to my parents' room to tell them what happened. My father told me sometimes dreams are so strong, they seem real. But it wasn't a dream, it was real, and she appeared night after night, for the last five years. I don't know how I'm supposed to help her, I don't know what she wants. She just keeps disappearing."

There was a moment of silence and the young girl exclaimed again with a heavy sigh, "I don't know what to do. I don't know what she wants!"

I looked at the worried young girl and said, "Why don't you ask her?"

Willie's Wake

This is a story of a ghost who attended his own wake. I'm assuming the ghost told someone about his problem and that someone passed it on until it was told to me. It's another Cape Breton story of a young man who went to the big city for a night on the town, unaware of what he was in for.

When William Whynott—known to his friends as Willie Boy—stepped off the curb, his mind was on something other than where he was stepping. One wrong move and it was over. Willie Boy never knew what hit him, feeling no pain, seeing only a burst of light and then darkness.

The next thing he knew he was sitting in his mother's parlour, surrounded by family and friends. Naturally, he wondered how on earth he'd gotten there. One moment he was stepping off a curb and the next moment he was back home. He just couldn't figure that one out. Was he dreaming? Willie Boy thought as much. What other explanation could there be? Willie Boy knew he was sitting on a chair but he also had the strangest feeling of being somewhere else in the room at the same time. And something else was confusing him, even irritating him. Why was everyone so quiet? You'd think they were attending a wake with all the sombre-looking faces. That must be it, he thought. But if that was so, then who had died?

Something else was bothering Willie Boy. Why was everyone staring at him? Some even touched his forehead with their fingers. Willie Boy thought that was the dumbest thing ever.

If he could just raise his head a bit. There it was again. That awful feeling of sitting and lying down at the same time.

There was a lot of movement behind him now. He could hear chairs being moved and people walking around the room, shaking hands, saying goodnight, and whispering that it was too bad he was gone. He was so young and such a nice young man. And then Willie Boy saw the undertaker coming into the room. He was right. Someone had died, but who? Just as soon as he got the chance he'd ask him.

Willie Boy nearly fell off his chair when out of nowhere the undertaker was peering down at him. How could that be? And then the undertaker reached across and began pulling down some kind of cover. Willie Boy tried to raise his arms off his chest to stop him but he just couldn't move them. He lay helpless as the cover closed over him. Willie Boy screamed and screamed, but no one heard him in the darkness.

Someone Else Is In My Grave!

Out of the blue, as the saying goes, a ghost suddenly appeared in a small New Brunswick community, causing great concern among the elders. The children, on the other hand, thought it was cool and suggested it would be good for tourism. Out of the mouths of babes, I guess.

The undertaker had received written instructions from an Alberta lawyer that the body of one Andrew Lassiter was to be buried under his supervision in the local cemetery. The undertaker met the train at the station, followed the instructions to the letter, and Mr. Lassiter's body was finally laid to rest. Or was it? Was there a connection between the ghost and the body of Mr. Lassiter? It was only five days later that the ghost made his debut appearance. Hmmm.

It was agreed by the village folk that you couldn't have a ghost popping up anywhere and at any hour of the day or night, no matter what the children said. After all, what did they know—they were only kids.

So a few of the braver souls were recruited to go to the graveyard and find out who the ghost was and why he was haunting their peaceful village. When the hastily-formed committee arrived at the cemetery the ghost was sitting on the grave of Andrew Lassiter. The ghost, they would later report, was quite old, perhaps in his late eighties. He was tall and lean and could easily have been a stand-in for Gary Cooper, wearing a long black coat that flapped in the wind when he stood. The grey hair under his black Stetson was thick and long.

The spokesman of the group took a deep breath and in a high-pitched voice told the ghost in no uncertain terms that the people of the village wanted to know who he was and why he was haunting the village. It must have been his high and mighty tone that did it. The ghost glared at the puny little man and disappeared without saying a word. The men hurried back to the village to report on what happened.

It was decided that an emergency meeting was necessary, and needless to say it was standing room only. The villagers came to hear how the elders were going to rid their village of this unwelcome apparition. The chairman reminded the meeting that since the clergy was unable to exorcise or banish the ghost for good, the floor was open to suggestions.

Before any hands were raised, however, the doors to the meeting hall burst open and young Roddie MacRey rushed in. Roddie told his neighbors that he himself had solved the mystery of the ghosts's presence. There was a lot of nodding and the hall was filled with an optimistic buzz. He continued, telling them that the solution had come to him in a dream. There was more vocalizing but this time it wasn't so enthusiastic. The chairman invited Roddie up on stage to enlighten everyone. Roddie told them that in his dream he'd been driving his team of horses over the old logging road past the cemetery when he'd seen the ghost standing by the gate. Roddie told them that the sight scared him nearly out of his wits, but when the ghost smiled and waved, he wasn't afraid anymore. Well, just a little bit, maybe.

"Then, rolling his eyes heavenward," Roddie said, "like a feather in a breeze, the ghost floated over to the wagon and plopped right down beside me." The ghost told Roddie that he had watched him driving his team of horses back and forth for several days and he could tell by the way he handled the animals that he was a kind and gentle person. He said he hoped that Roddie would, if asked, help someone with a life and death problem even if that person was a ghost. Roddie nodded that if he could, he would. With that, the ghost told Roddie who he was and why he was haunting such a nice place.

The ghost told young Roddie his name was Andrew Lassiter. He said he was raised in an orphanage just outside the village. On his sixteenth birthday, he left New Brunswick and for a time worked in the lumber camps of northern Ontario. When he saved enough money he moved west and eventually settled in Cold Lake, Alberta, where he lived until he and twenty-five passengers died in a head-on collision between their tour bus and a truck. The ghost said the last thing he remembered was an explosion and fire. There was a long pause before the ghost continued. He went on to relate that he had requested in his will that his body be returned to the village for burial. With a deep sigh, he told Roddie that the body in the coffin was not his but that of his close friend Ian McFayden, who was on the tour with him.

"We were two close friends who didn't have a living relative to our names, and rather than sitting in some nursing home staring into space, we decided to see the world or the country at least. Just before the accident, Ian, who was recovering from the flu, felt a chill so we exchanged jackets, mine being much warmer. When rescuers found our bodies we were still wearing each other's jackets and when the police checked the identification we were carrying—well, need I say more? Ian's in my grave and I'm in his."

After hearing Roddie's story, the good folk attending the meeting began to see the ghost in a different light. There was now a degree of empathy in their souls.

It took a while but Roddie kept his promise to Andrew Lassiter's ghost and the mixup was eventually corrected by the appropriate people. Andrew is finally resting in his own grave. And in Cold Lake, Alberta, Ian is in his. So far Andrew Lassiter has kept his word. He is no longer haunting the village. Andrew's friend Ian McFayden, however, is another matter. Oh well, another story, perhaps for another time.

The Piano

*H*ere is another story from Joyce Cook, a favourite of hers. It's the story of a sea captain, his lovely wife, and a grand piano.

The captain often brought his young wife presents from his journeys across the ocean, but he had never returned with a certain thing she wished for. Being a stubborn one, she reminded him that the best gift he could bring back from a faraway place was a piano.

During an afternoon stroll through London's shopping district, the captain remembered his wife's wish. So, he purchased a lovely grand piano and had it brought on board his ship.

On the return to his home port of North West Cove, however, the ship and all on board were caught in a terrible storm. All hands were lost along with the vessel and its cargo.

However, when the wind is just right and the time is exact, if you happen to be at North West Cove, you may hear the sounds of a piano playing somewhere beneath the sea. Some people have, I'm told.

The Ring

*R*obyn Slater never slept in, but she woke one morning with a shock to see that the clock on the bedside dresser read 8:40 A.M. Could she make the sailing on time? Her ship was scheduled to leave South Hampton at 10:00 A.M. If she hurried, she still might make it. Thank God, she thought, the trunk and large suitcases were sent on ahead.

The taxi driver reassured her, "Don't worry, we'll make it on time."

With just minutes to spare, Robyn raced down the long terminal to pier 13. She heard the ship's whistle in the distance. Was she going to make it? It would definitely be close.

Suddenly she saw a young man, a soldier, fall to the hard concrete floor ahead of her. Robyn looked around but there was no one else nearby to help. She knelt down and took the young man's hand, telling him she would hurry on ahead and get help. He shook his head, and his face was wet with tears. He squeezed her hand one long moment, then closed his eyes forever. The silence was broken by the whistle of the passenger liner leaving the dock for the long voyage across the Atlantic.

When the attendants closed the doors to the ambulance and drove off, Robyn became aware that she was holding a ring in her hand.

How did that get there? It must have come off the young soldier's finger while she was holding his hand. There could be no other possible explanation. Her mind on other things, she dropped the ring in her coat pocket and forgot about it. She was still wrapped up in the incredible events of the day as well as her apprehension about her new travel arrangements. Although she was petrified of flying, she had no choice but to book a flight back to Canada.

Two nights later, she was safely home watching television with her grandmother. The program was interrupted by a news bulletin, a tragedy: Ocean liner collided with another ship. Of the 1,200 passengers on board, only 250 survived the cold Atlantic waters.

It was the vessel she'd missed on the morning the soldier had died in her arms. Robyn was shaken by the news and couldn't speak. She sat there trembling, wondering if she might have been one of the victims had she not missed the boat. Was it a blessing in disguise? Did fate play a hand in it?

Her grandmother helped her upstairs to lie down and rest. Putting Robyn's earrings on the bureau, her grandmother noticed a familiar-looking ring. She picked it up and studied it very carefully before asking her granddaughter, "Where did you get this ring?"

"Oh, remember," Robyn replied, "when I stopped to help the young soldier—the ring mysteriously ended up in my hand. It must have slipped off his finger when I was holding him. Why do you ask?"

Tears welling up in her eyes, Robyn's grandmother told her that as a young girl she had given a ring to a boy going off to war. They had agreed not to get married until he returned. "This ring was the bond between us, but it was not to be. He was killed during the Normandy invasion! He came back to save you!"

watch where You sleep

John and Mary were late getting away from Cape Breton on their annual vacation, and they found all the mainland campgrounds filled. Around two in the morning, Mary pointed to a small knoll up ahead and suggested that it would be a suitable place to spend the night. They were in bed for only a few minutes when the RV began to shake violently and the night sounds were drowned out by a deep moaning. They rushed outside to check, but found nothing—all was calm and quiet. They returned to the RV and were no sooner back in bed when it started again. Needless to say, they remained sitting up outside for the rest of the night. In the morning, Mary noticed a plaque as they drove off the knoll:

Keep Off
Indian burial ground

The Lovely Ghost of May Day, 1829

And also from the late Elsie Churchill Tolson's book, this tragic but true story of young love and tragedy.

Around 1829 in the merry month of May, handsome young Henry Montague arrived in Halifax to visit Mary Lawrence from Windsor, where he had just completed his studies at King's College. Mary, a lovely young lady of 17, was to marry Henry just as soon as he received his church appointment.

Mary was radiantly happy and Henry felt like the luckiest man in the world. Halifax was at the time a sociable town and the popular couple was immediately swept along in a succession of parties. Their friend Mr. Berryman suggested a "Maying" party at Bedford, and Mary and Henry accepted his invitation gladly. The young ladies, wearing long frocks and wide-brimmed leghorn hats, were called for by gentlemen in horse-drawn wagons.

At 6:30 A.M. they drove along "the romantic road that winds around the basin" as far as Ten Mile House. They turned right and followed a narrow road to the Manor House and from there, through the fields of the Sackville estate farm as far as Parker's Brook, where the Parker Brook Bridge on Shore Drive is now.

They walked up the side of Parker's brook about a mile until they arrived at Lily Lake, the men carrying baskets and a small canoe. Mary called out, "What a pleasant place for our picnic. Let us have it under the old beech tree."

They deposited their heavy loads and began to search for mayflowers. The girls made a wreath of the pink blossoms and, by unanimous consent, crowned Mary the Queen of the May. Then they all joined hands and danced around Mary singing the May Song.

The men had caught some trout and built a fire, allowing it to burn to red embers, then circled it with fish on peeled alder sticks stuck in the ground which they kept turning until the fish were barbecued. The girls spread the picnic and sat down prettily. The men did the serving, helping the girls to pieces of fish and making them laugh so much that the hills echoed. They played games, sang songs, and told stories.

Mr. Berryman offered to take Mary and Miss Martin in the canoe to the middle of the lake to pick lilies. As he was paddling, he made a sudden turn, unaware that Mary had been reaching for a lily. She lost her balance and plunged into the water, while those on shore shouted at the sight. The shock dazed Mr. Berryman for a moment, but he ripped off his coat and dove in. Alas, Mary could not swim and her long dress, heavy with water, pulled her below the surface at once.

Henry could not swim either, but raced frantically into the lake through the tangled weeds and lilies. His friends ran after him and had a difficult time holding him back.

Berryman searched until he was exhausted but could not find Mary. Meanwhile, some of the men had run back to Bedford for help, then drove the horses to Halifax to get dragging equipment. They arrived back in three hours but nothing was ever seen again of the lovely Mary Lawrence.

Henry was inconsolable. He moved to Europe, but in many years he could not forget, so he returned to Bedford and walked to Lily Lake. There he sat beneath the old beech tree indulging his grief until evening shadows darkened.

Suddenly a brightness passed over the water. He lifted his eyes as "round the lake light music stole" and saw Mary's ghost glide, smiling o'er the fatal waters.

The vision passed like a shooting star into the darkness of the woods beyond. Henry, already worn out with grief and suffering, died a week later and was buried in the churchyard of St. John's Anglican Church in Sackville.

A Mr. Jourdrey who lived near the lake told Mrs. Tolson that when he was a child, he and other children were taken to the lake on May Day to watch for the light and the lovely ghost of Mary Lawrence!

The Lady with the Candle

*T*his is the story of a weeping young maiden who has been seen carrying a candle. An old fisherman, sitting in his rowboat some distance from shore, saw her coming down to the water's edge. He slumped down in the boat, hoping she couldn't see him. He should have known that you can't hide from spirits, but she paid him no heed. He peered over the gunwale, watching as she climbed the jagged rocks to stand there staring out to sea. He thinks she was longing for a lost love. A strong wind coming off the shore should have blown out the candle she was holding, but the flame didn't even flicker.

The Little Black Dress

*L*ittle Jennifer was a blue-eyed blonde, while Victoria had raven hair and eyes so dark it was difficult to tell their colour. They met on the first day of kindergarten and became inseparable, "the bestest of friends."

While Jennifer was born into wealth, Victoria grew up in a loving but modest home. She couldn't believe how many beautiful clothes her friend owned. Her favourite was Jennifer's little black dress. One day, she too would own such a beautiful dress.

The phone call came late at night. Jennifer's father stood in silence as he listened, and when he hung up, his wife was standing in the doorway waiting to find out who was calling at such an hour.

"It was Victoria's father," he told her in a daze, "The police believe it was a hit and run. Victoria's body was found by the side of the road."

When her parents broke the news of Victoria's death, Jennifer collapsed in her father's arms. She told her parents that she wanted her friend to wear her little black dress to heaven. "Victoria would like that," her mother agreed.

After the funeral, Jennifer retired early and next morning told her mother that Victoria had come to her in a dream. "She told me not to mourn; that she is happy and will always watch over me."

When Jennifer left for school, her mother went up to her daughter's room to tidy up. She opened the closet door, and there hanging on the rack was Jennifer's little black dress.

The Ghost in the Empty Grave

One morning while checking my mail I recognized the familiar handwriting of my friend, the late author Edith Mosher. The story she enclosed has a surprising and humorous ending, a reminder that things are not always what they seem.

This little gem happened in the village of Summerville, Nova Scotia, over a hundred years ago and it's about two young lads who enjoyed hanging out at the general store in the evenings, listening to the older men telling tall tales.

An elderly man in the village had died and his burial was scheduled to take place the next morning. Naturally, the death was a topic of conversation around the general store's pot-bellied stove. When the two young men were leaving, an elderly man told them with a smile that it was fortunate the boys didn't live on the far side of the hill. If they did, they'd have to pass the graveyard where perhaps the ghost of the old man might be on the prowl.

Once outside and away from the taunts of the older men, the boys convinced each other that they weren't afraid of any ghost, new or old. In fact, they insisted, they didn't even believe in such things. Full of bravado, they challenged each other to walk up the hill straight through the graveyard and past the old man's grave. They entered the darkened graveyard where they found a new grave close to the fence. There was a mound of earth by the grave, and beside it lay a rough box.

The boys weren't feeling nearly as brave as they had when climbing the hill. A strong wind began to pick up and a crescent moon hung low in the western sky. One of the young men joked to hide his fear and said, "What would you do if the old man popped up from that box right now?"

As if by magic, or something even more mysterious, a shadowy white form rose up from the empty grave, hung there briefly, let out a shrilling sound, and sank back down again. Both young boys froze in their tracks. Again the thing appeared, and again the terrible wailing.

The boys fled as fast as they could back down the hill to the general store where they collapsed in front of the older men. When they caught their breath enough to speak, they described what they'd seen in the graveyard. Most of the men laughed at the story, but a curious few decided to go to the graveyard and see for themselves, insisting that the boys go with them. As they neared the graveyard, though, even the skeptics were shaken by the awful sound.

With lanterns raised high, the men checked the open grave and the mystery was solved. What they saw was more farm animal than phantom. On the other side of the newly-dug grave, a wire fence separated the graveyard from a pasture. Sometime after the gravediggers had left, an old sheep had gotten though the fence and fallen into the open grave.

After the animal was lifted out of the grave and put over the fence, it promptly left the scene. As did the two young boys, feeling rather "sheepish," you might say.

Chapter Six

Malice, Mayhem, and Missing Persons

Something Else Entirely

One morning while in the Halifax International Airport, an apologetic stranger sat down beside me and in time passed on this little horror story. It's become an urban legend.

She was young and pretty and went to bed early with her canine protector lying beside her bed. Sometime during the night she was awakened by a strange sound. The pretty young thing lay motionless, listening. All she could hear was the heavy breathing of her dog and the wind outside. Before going back to sleep, she reached down and petted her dog's head. In turn, she felt the warm moisture of the dog's tongue as it licked her hand. Believing that nothing could harm her while her dog was by her bedside, she smiled and closed her eyes.

In the morning when she pulled back the shower curtain, there hanging by a cord was her dog. On the medicine cabinet mirror, a scrawled message read: Remember that humans can also lick hands.

The Second-hand Bed

"There," exclaimed the boy's parents, "a bed of your own. No more complaining about sharing a bed with your younger brother."

The bed they had bought for their eldest son was a second-hand one. The owner of the store told them he bought it at an auction up-country. It was stored, according to the seller, in the attic of an old farmhouse.

Sometime around midnight the young lad was awakened by the sound of someone crying. He swore that the sound was coming from the bed itself. Before he could get his feet on the floor, the bed began to rise and went flying across the room.

In the morning, his parents found the bed overturned and their son huddled in the corner mumbling about a ghost in the bed. When he calmed down enough to tell them what had happened, his parents drove to the farming community where the auction had been held. They learned that the farmer and his wife sold everything and moved away after their daughter was mysteriously murdered while she slept.

"Yes," the auctioneer said, "the bed you bought was hers."

The parents did not sell the second-hand bed. They chopped it up for firewood. But what about the ghost?

The Whitzman Mystery

*F*riday the thirteenth was an unlucky day for 43-year-old Benny Whitzman of Halifax. On that day in 1953, he closed his grocery store and set out under a light snow to hunt rabbits along the St. Margaret's Bay Road, never to be seen again. On that fateful afternoon, four-foot-tall Benny was wearing a red hunting cap, a red jacket, breeches, and high leather boots, carrying a 12 gauge shotgun over his shoulder. Dressed like that and carrying a shotgun, he would have been hard to miss.

So, what happened to this diminutive businessman on that cold winter afternoon? Did he become disorientated in the growing darkness? Did panic drive him further and further into the woods? Probably not. Benny was an experienced hunter and knew how to survive in the wild.

The RCMP file shows that Benny was picked up around 3:00 P.M. by a motorist who dropped Benny off near Fraser's sawmill near

Timberlea on the Bay Road. Benny must have spent about an hour hunting there because another motorist also gave him a ride, dropping him off closer to Halifax on the Greenhead Road near Lakeside.

Around 5:00 P.M. a taxi driver spotted Benny hitchhiking in the direction of Halifax. The taxi driver made a mental note to give Benny a lift into Halifax after he'd dropped off his fare. That, according to the police report, was the last time Benny was seen alive.

When Benny didn't return home that evening, his family notified the police who tried to pinpoint where Benny had last been seen. Several people reported seeing Benny in several locations, and his family and friends searched most of the night. The search was made more difficult by a steady snowfall—whatever tracks there might have been were quickly covered by the snow.

Two days later, the RCMP entered the search, joined by three brothers—Joe, Bernard, and Sonny Day, who knew the thick woods of Lakeside like their own backyard. They, too, came up empty-handed and a much larger search party—including many Lakeside residents and members of the Lakeside volunteer fire department—was organized.

Benny Whitzman was a flashy little man. He may have been small in stature but he knew how to stand out in a crowd, wearing expensive clothes and jewellery. On the day he went missing, he was wearing two valuable rings—one of gold and the other diamond—as well as an expensive wristwatch.

One of the Day brothers thinks he may have been murdered for his jewellery. "Done in for his diamond ring." Benny's cousin David Whitzman says, "No one knows what really happened. It's a swampy area. He got lost and probably stepped into a sump hole."

In the end, it's as if Benny Whitzman simply disappeared from the face of the earth—or was swallowed by it.

The Bait

The fishermen who told me this whopper couldn't help but chuckle.

"So, it's decided then," Lauchie said to his wife, "We'll leave early in the morning, and that way we'll arrive at the camp before dark."

Robyn nodded happily. She was, to say the least, surprised that her husband had invited her along on a weekend fishing trip. It was something he had never done before. Why the change of heart now?

Robyn's love of fishing went all the way back to her childhood when she and her father would spend their Saturday afternoons fly-fishing. Those were special times she would always treasure. Robyn still kept the red and blue polka dot kerchief her father wore whenever he went fishing. She would wear it tomorrow for good luck.

Still, the invitation was unexpected and she stole glances at her husband. She tried to study his face to see if there was anything different, anything she hadn't noticed before.

Lauchie was also thinking, finalizing the plan he had worked on for months. After weighing all the options and risks, he'd decided that a boating accident would be the best way. No tell-tale evidence, no marks or bruises, nothing to come back later to haunt him.

It was dark when they arrived at the cabin, and Lauchie started a fire while Robyn prepared supper. It was a pleasant evening, but lying in bed later, Robyn was overcome by an irrational fear. It swept through her like a cold, wet wind. Lauchie's bulk lay beside her, fast asleep and snoring. But for some unknown reason, Robyn slept fitfully that night.

It was nearly 6:00 A.M. when she got out of bed. She could hear Lauchie moving around in the kitchen, and the aroma of freshly brewed coffee filled the small cabin. Robyn chalked her night fears up to her imagination.

A dense fog hung over the river, and Robyn suggested that they wait until the fog lifted. But Lauchie, shoving the boat away from the wharf, insisted that he knew the river like the back of his hand. Huddled in the bow, Robyn sat watching as Lauchie's powerful arms moved in sure, swift strokes, rowing them farther out into the river.

After an hour without so much as a nibble, Lauchie suggested they change places. "Careful," he told Robyn as she stepped toward the stern. They met in the middle of the boat, and Lauchie's strong arms folded around her. Before she knew what was happening, she was hurtling headlong into the dark water below. She came up gasping for air, and felt a hand firmly clasped on her head. It was Lauchie, thank God, he was rescuing her. But he didn't lift her back in the boat. He pushed her back down, holding her head under the water. She fought desperately, but Lauchie was too strong. Finally she couldn't hold her breath any longer and descended into blackness.

The police called it a boating accident. Lauchie told them that before the terrible tragedy, he hadn't been feeling well and decided to lie down. Robyn had wanted to try her luck, however, and Lauchie had told her to be careful. When she failed to return he'd become concerned and called the police. Robyn's body was never found. Just the empty boat.

Two years and a ten million dollar life insurance windfall later, Lauchie returned to the scene of the crime—something many murderers do. Lauchie had ambitious plans for the camp. Now that he could afford it, he wanted to build a more lavish summer home on the same site with an elaborate dock to accommodate the luxury boat he had his eye on.

On the way back to the cabin, a powerful urge to try his luck at fishing came over him. Why not, he thought, it's been awhile. He was overcome by a strange, almost hypnotic feeling, as if someone was telling him to wade out instead of using the boat. Lauchie was now waist-deep in the river. He took a step forward and was about to cast his line when he felt himself sinking. He had heard about such things—a sinkhole or quicksand. Now he was alone. There was no one to hear his cries for help. The more he fought to get free, the deeper he sank. Just before he disappeared below the surface, Lauchie caught sight of a familiar red and blue polka dot kerchief floating by.

The River Ghost

*F*or every twist and turn of the river, there's a story to be told. And along the rugged coastline of Nova Scotia, there are many mysteries that still haunt those drawn to its shores. This one involves a woman who strolled one afternoon along the banks of the river. Not long into her walk, the sun disappeared behind a storm cloud and a thick bank of fog swept over the water.

The young woman stopped and listened, wondering if she was hearing things. No, there it was again—someone crying for help. More clearly now, a woman's voice coming from somewhere out in the middle of the river, or perhaps from the other side. Oars splashed against the water, and out of the fog an old man in a small boat slowly rowed toward her. His head was bent low and his cap was nearly pulled over his eyes.

The woman slipped down the bank, told the old man she had heard someone in trouble on the other side, and asked him to please take her across. The old man nodded but said nothing as the woman got into the boat. When they were halfway across, the cries for help started anew. About to ask the old man if he heard the voice as well, she noticed a blue kerchief tied around his neck, partially obscuring a hideous scar. In a raspy voice the old man said, "I, too, have heard those screams many times. She is the ghost of a young woman who was murdered on this river many years ago. Her murderer was eventually caught and hanged, but neither the victim nor her murderer can find peace."

When the woman reported what she had seen and heard to the police, the officer smiled and asked if the old man had a raspy voice and a scar on his neck, much like a rope burn. When she left the police station she understood. She was in the wrong place at the wrong time, caught up in the torment of that other world.

Desilda's Cries

Edmond Chatfield and Desilda St. Clair, a couple from the state of Maine, were out sailing one long weekend back in the early 1800s. Caught in a violent storm, they ended up shipwrecked on Grand Manan Island. Awaiting rescue, they discovered to their horror that the island was used by pirates. Hiding in the woods, they observed these cutthroats burying their booty. Both were caught by the riff-raff and poor Edmond was hanged from the nearest tree while his beloved Desilda was forced to watch.

Edmond was lucky. Desilda was not. She was raped and beaten time and again until the pirates were through with her and set upon her with rocks, sending her half-crazed into the forest. Desilda may have been half out of her mind, but she was going to avenge the death of her beloved Edmond. One by one, she enticed the rabble into the woods where she crushed their skulls with boulders.

To this very day, some will say, the ghosts of Edmond and Desilda can be seen roaming the island. Edmond races about as a headless ghost while Desilda, who eventually went insane and died before being rescued, is seen and heard screaming the name of her beloved.

The Flaming Maiden

*A*nd then there is the spirit of the Indian maiden who is seen standing in the waters of Indian Harbour. With head and arms raised heavenward, she is consumed by fire and her ashes are carried out to sea.

The story of the Indian maiden is a true Maritime Mystery simply because no one knows what happened to her. Her death, however, must have been a violent one, one that involved fire. Such a tragic spectacle certainly fires the imagination, though. Perhaps she was murdered, or perhaps her wigwam was set on fire by a mad trapper.

Hannah Gibb

*W*hat I'm about to relate happened in the mid-1700s in a Maritime seafaring community. Where? No one knows, exactly. This, is what happened to Hannah Gibb, a young lady of breathtaking beauty with long, glowing black hair that rippled in waves down her back as she walked. When she entered a room, all eyes were on her.

One evening Hannah was late leaving her aunt's home. She hurriedly kissed her aunt goodbye, pulled the shawl tight around her head, grabbed a lantern to guide her way, and hurried along the shore to her family's cottage a mile away. Rolling clouds raced across the face of the moon casting eerie shadows on the water. The coming darkness was making it difficult for Hannah to see.

She stopped suddenly. Was there someone up ahead? Someone waiting? She raised the lamp higher and peered into the darkness trying to see who it was. Her heart sank. It was a sailor.

"Oh, God," she prayed, "let him not be from one of the pirate ships." The hand holding the lamp froze in midair. Hannah dug her toes into the sand, but her legs wouldn't move. The sailor took a deep drink from a bottle, threw it down, and came at her.

When Hannah failed to arrive home, a search party was organized. Her aunt told the authorities, "yes, it was getting late when Hannah left and from my door I watched her walk along the shore for quite a while. When she was nearly out of sight, I assumed everything to be alright and went back inside."

Next morning, investigators found two sets of footprints in the sand made by a man's boots and the bare feet of a woman. The prints showed a struggle then disappeared at the water's edge indicating that someone had been dragged by their heels, probably into a boat. A broken lantern and an empty rum bottle were found, but not a trace of Hannah Gibb anywhere.

Three months later and five miles from Hannah Gibbs' home, two children were throwing rocks off a cliff into the foaming surf below when they saw a body being pushed in and out by the surf. It was the body of Hannah Gibb! The only marks were bruises around her neck—the marks of strangulation. There was something else. Her beautiful hair was gone. Why, everyone asked, was her hair cut off?

Days later, the owner of a local inn told authorities that he had overheard the leader of a gang of cutthroats telling other layabouts of how his captain had kidnapped a fair maiden and taken her aboard ship.

"Ol' Capt'n Clive, he dragged her into his cabin but the silly wench tried to get away and he was forced to do her in. When the vessel was far enough off the coast, Capt'n Clive dumped her over the side, but not before he cut off the wench's pretty locks. Next morning, he came on deck with two fishbone braids of the young thing's hair attached to his own. The kind that hang down, Indian-like. He sure loved them braids.

"But it was her lovely hair what did him in. We found him, eyes bulging out of his sockets, dead as can be. While he slept, the wench's locks got twisted tight around his neck and strangled him."

A New Ross Mystery

*T*he death of a child from natural causes is a heart-breaking loss for any parent, but to have a child vanish forever without explanation is truly a living nightmare. Haunting questions must plague those parents every single day of their lives. The hardest part of all is not knowing what really happened.

That is the sad story of the Meister family of New Ross and their son Fred, aged seven, who walked away from the protection of his parents' arms one spring afternoon.

It was a Saturday in 1908, just past noon and opening day of the trout season. The Meister children set off to visit their uncle's farm two miles away to try their luck at their favourite fishing hole. Their mother had a premonition, a heavy foreboding, and she didn't want the children to go near the swollen river. She told her sons that the spring run-off and heavy rains had made the river too dangerous for them. Fred and his older brother Ira promised their mother they would stay away from the river, and they headed off for their uncle's farm.

Near mid-afternoon Fred, Ira, and their cousins became restless and, against their mother's wishes, went into the woods towards the Larder River to try their luck.

The fish weren't biting though, so eventually the boys decided to return to their uncle's farm. However, they met their 15-year-old cousin Terry on the way back, and he persuaded Fred to stay at the river with him. After about an hour, Fred complained that he was cold, tired, and wanted to go home. Terry wanted to stay, so he walked Fred some distance, then warned him to stay on the road and not to turn at the fork that leads into Ross Marsh.

Seven-year-old Fred Meister, wearing a cap, a bright red sweater, and a pair of larrigans (a type of moccasin), set off by himself for home, never to be seen again.

Storm clouds began to form and darkness descended on the community of New Ross. The Meister parents became concerned. Where was Fred? Word spread quickly through the community that the boy was lost in the woods. A search party about two hundred strong was immediately organized.

The job was made nearly impossible by one of the worst storms in the history of Lunenburg County. The voices calling Fred's name were drowned out by the vicious thunder, and beyond one set of footprints in the mud, the rain washed away any trace of the boy. The search party combed the woods and the river throughout the rest of the night and all the next day, but in the end, there was not a single trace of Fred anywhere. It was as if he vanished from the earth, or was swallowed up by it.

The frantic Meister family was not spared the con artists who take advantage of such situations. In desperation, the Meisters even paid a fortune teller who insisted she knew where Fred was. But still, no sign of their son.

Rex Meister was born three years after his brother's disappearance. As Rex grew up, he too fished the Larder River and his thoughts were often on the brother he never knew. Rex Meister hoped that someday he would come upon a piece of red sweater, a buckle or moccasin, perhaps even the remains of his lost brother.

Terry Meister, the last person to see little Fred alive, maintained to the end that Fred simply got lost and it cost him his life. Rex, however, believes Terry was responsible. He was much older and should have stayed with Fred until he was safely on the main road home.

Now in his late eighties, Rex Meister sits by the window of his New

Ross home and stares off into the woods beyond, wondering what happened on that day so long ago. Not far from the Meister home is the New Ross cemetery. On a good day, Rex visits the family graves. One remains empty and the tombstone bears the name of Fred Meister. Rex still hopes that someday someone will find Fred's remains and reunite him with his family at last.

The Pickled Remains

This is the story of a carpenter, his money, and his wife. We'll call the couple Ezra and Matilda, and it was Ezra who built the first gallows in St. Andrews, New Brunswick.

Old Ezra didn't trust Matilda with his savings, so he took the money and hid it. When Ezra was out of the house, Matilda searched high and low until she found the booty. 'One good turn deserves another,' Matilda thought, so she stashed it away.

Ezra came home, found the money gone, and demanded Matilda tell him where she hid it. When she refused, he up and killed her right there on the spot. Ezra chopped Matilda into little pieces and stuffed her parts in a large pickle barrel, hiding the dastardly deed in the dark cellar.

Ezra didn't get away with murdering his wife, of course. His tongue betrayed him, or perhaps the liquor that passed over it. Over drinks with his cronies, he bragged that he'd done his wife in. The police were notified and they found Matilda's parts well-preserved in pickle juice.

Guilty was the verdict and Ezra was hanged. Hanged on the very gallows he built.

Chapter Seven

Family Ties

The Miner's Ghost

*M*rs. John McNeil was the wife of a Cape Breton miner. One warm summer afternoon while crossing a field on her way to fetch her cow, she met her neighbour who was on a similar mission. While the ladies stopped to pass the time of day, Mrs. McNeil happened to glance toward the back door of her home and saw her husband going inside.

"Strange," she told her neighbour, "my husband just went inside the house. Maybe he's sick or there's something wrong at the mine. Anyway, he's home and that's all that matters. I'll fetch the cow later."

Her neighbor said she'd bring the cow home when she fetched her own. On the way back, the neighbor saw her own husband standing in the doorway and she asked why he was home from the mine so early.

"The mine," he said, "was shut down, because John McNeil was killed."

When his wife recovered, she asked what time the tragedy had occurred. When he told her, she realized that was the exact moment when Mrs. McNeil saw her husband arrive home.

On Thin Ice

*T*ommy's mother was always cautioning him about skating on thin ice. "Especially spring ice," she'd say, then mutter something about rotting underneath. But this wasn't spring. It was winter, and Tommy couldn't wait to try out the new skates he'd gotten for Christmas.

Of course, mother would say he was tempting fate. She would say, "The winter will be long and you'll have plenty of time to go skating on the lake." Then she'd give a deep sigh and mutter, "Boys."

Tommy's home was located on a hill overlooking the lake that he secretly thought of as his own. His bedroom window faced the lake and he would sit at the window waiting for it to freeze over fully.

In the last week of December, he decided he couldn't wait any longer. Of course, he knew what his mother would say—"It's too early. Just look, there are still ducks swimming in parts of the lake. Be patient, you'll have lots of time to go skating."

So he didn't tell her. He slipped past the kitchen where his family was talking, and out the front door. He raced down to the lake with his brand new skates swung over his shoulder and wasted little time in lacing them to his feet. Young Tommy sped off on that mirror of shimmering ice, feeling free as a bird with the wind in his face. What was his mother so worried about, anyway? The ice under his skates was hard and strong, and why shouldn't he skate straight across to the other side of the lake? It wasn't even a mile. With the wind at his back, Tommy knew he could make it across and back before supper.

The shock of the cold December water forced Tommy to gasp in a deep breath. The cold lasted only an instant before he felt a calming feeling come over him. He drifted down, down, rolling over and over. He felt light-headed, like a bird in flight.

When he awakened, he was surprised to find himself safely back in his own bedroom. Beyond his window, he heard voices hollering instruction and he could see the flash of a red light bouncing off the window. When he looked outside, he was surprised and startled to see people racing back and forth from the house to the lake. Out on the lake there were more people gathered around a hole in the ice. Tommy watched the men lift something from the water, place it on a sled, and bring it to a waiting ambulance.

Tommy sat on the bed and had the strangest feeling about the boy in the ambulance.

After Tommy's body was taken away, his mother went up to his room to be alone with her son's familiar things. She noticed wet footprints going down the narrow hall and disappearing at Tommy's bedroom door.

A Ghostly Pair

I was comfortably seated in the very last row of my favourite Halifax theatre, the Oxford, waiting for the movie to start, when I felt a hand touch my shoulder. "Hi Bill," said a voice in a low whisper. "My name is Bob Kitson. Loved your book. Got a minute?"

"Sure," I said.

He sat in the seat in front of me, draped his arm over the top, entwined his fingers, and told me his favourite native New Brunswick ghost story. If I remember correctly, it took place in the early 1900s.

Identical twins, the two girls were in their early twenties and they were inseparable. Lovers of the outdoor life, they set out one weekend on a hiking trip. When they failed to return home, a search party set out to find them.

After an exhausting night of searching, their bodies were found just before dawn in a hastily-dug grave. Their murderer was never caught.

Not long after the murders, reports began circulating of a blonde girl appearing mysteriously where the bodies had been found. Everyone agreed that she couldn't be the ghost of one of the murdered twins because in life they were rarely apart. Surely, it was agreed, in death they would be inseparable. But if the ghost was indeed one of the identical twins, then which one was she?

"How's that for a mystery?" he commented.

"Yeah," I said, "some mystery."

The lights went down and we turned our attention to the celluloid world of make-believe.

watching Over Me

While in hospital recovering from two major heart attacks, Harold Nickerson of Harrietsfield, Nova Scotia had the comforting presence of his good wife by his bedside. While recuperating at home, Mr. Nickerson was awakened from a sound sleep to see Mrs. Nickerson sitting on the side of his bed watching over him. Only one thing amiss—his good wife had been dead for nearly five years!

There was another strange occurrence in the Nickerson household. When Harold's daughter and her new husband looked over their wedding pictures, who else do you think was in the photograph? The bride's grandmother, of course. Though, when the wedding picture was taken, granny Nickerson was twelve years dead!

I guess it runs in the family.

The spirit within

Clayton Colpitts does not scoff at such things because he himself has felt the presence of a loved one long after their death. After his wife Jessie died, Clayton insists that his wife's spirit continued to inhabit not only their home, but also the body of his constant companion—pet dog Brendy.

You cannot convince Clayton Colpitts otherwise, and why should anyone try?

A Relative Ghost

This story was passed on to me by a Pictonian during a book signing. It was suggested that I get in touch with Corie Allen who had a surprising and spirited tale to tell. Corie lives in Blue Mountain, Nova Scotia, and one of his passions is to ride his motorcycle through the many trails in the Blue Mountain range.

Corie and his cousin were biking along a dense wooded area one afternoon when they saw, just up ahead, a heavily bearded old man standing in the middle of the trail with a woodsman's axe in his hands. According to Corie, the stranger wore typical lumberjack clothing, right down to the high boots. What to do! Should they turn their bikes and speed off the other way? Or should they stand their ground? The old man made no attempt to move, standing there as if he was in some kind of trance. Finally, Corie decided to drive past the stranger praying nothing would happen. As the two young bikers came closer, the old man stood looking straight ahead. Corie and his cousin rode past the old man without incident. When they were a half-mile away, they stopped and tried to figure out who he was, agreeing that if they didn't go back they would always wonder. But when they returned, the old man was gone.

Corie arrived home and told his family about seeing an old man on the trail. When he described what the stranger wore and looked like, Corie's grandfather raised his head and for a moment said nothing. Then, speaking directly to his grandson, he said, "The man you described was my father, your great-grandfather, who died a long time before you were born."

To this day the Allen family wonders why he came back.

The Fox River Ghost

There is a small community near Port Greville called Fox River, where Clayton Colpitts' late father-in-law lived. Mr. Colpitts told me about his father-in-law's first wife, who kept coming back from the grave. She died at 27 and left her husband to raise four young children—two boys and two girls.

In time, Clayton's father-in-law began courting another woman. One evening while returning home, he saw a woman standing in front of his house. He told his lady friend to wait by the gate while he went to investigate. When he got closer, he saw the ghost of his wife standing by the kitchen door. They stood silently staring at each other, but when he moved closer to speak to her, she turned and disappeared around the corner of the house.

About a week later the two young daughters were playing with their cousins in an old abandoned house, when one of the girls—Ethel—decided to explore the upstairs. When she reached the top landing, she screamed and ran down and out of the house with her sister and cousin right behind her. At home she told her father that her mother was standing in the doorway at the top of the stairs. Clayton says his father-in-law believed the ghost of his dead wife meant no harm. She was merely watching over her family.

The Haunting of Mrs. Dean

*A*while back I received a letter from Mrs. Shirley G. Dean of River Hebert, Nova Scotia. She told me that there was a time when she had laughed at people who claimed their homes were haunted—but not anymore!

She never believed in such things until ten years ago, two years after her husband died. She began seeing his face at the back door very plain for a long time almost every day, usually between 3:00 and 3:30 P.M. and mostly on rainy days. One day, she called her sister-in-law over and asked her to look at the back door. She looked out and said, "Oh, so and so, don't do that." That was when Mrs. Dean knew it wasn't in her imagination, and her sister-in-law refused to come back to the house again for a long time.

It wasn't the end for Mrs. Dean, though. "I told a friend about it and she said I wouldn't see him no more, but I would hear him from then on."

"Some time after that in the middle of the night I heard sawing in the basement. Next morning my sister-in-law came over at eleven. We both saw sawdust by the sawhorse. It startled her and when she spoke, the sawdust vanished. When I got up in the morning there had been molasses spilled on the table with a dish sitting in the middle of the molasses.

"Some time after that my sister and her husband came down from Amherst. Her husband went down the basement for something and while he was there, something came out of the spare bedroom. My sister asked me if I had seen it. I said, 'yes,' but it moved too fast for me to see what it was.

"Some time after that I woke up in the middle of the night; I could feel someone in the bed alongside of me. I got out of bed quick and went over to my sister-in-law's and stayed there for the night.

"The third week in May, I was humming, making a stew; I had the meat, turnips, carrots, peas, and green beans pretty well cooked. I just nicely got the potatoes and barley put in the pot when I heard a terrible racket in the front room. I took off out the back door. A half hour later I got the guts to go back in and I called my stepdaughter to drop everything and come up. When I hung up the phone I took the shakes and went back outdoors. My stepdaughter came up and said, 'What are you doing out with no coat on? It's a cold day.'

"We went in the house. My stew had boiled all over the stove. We checked all the rooms and the attic and basement. Nothing was out of place. We shut the stove off and we went to see the doctor. The doctor put the stethoscope in his ears; the other end was over two feet from me and we could hear my heart beat. The heartbeat was that loud. He gave me a pill to put under my tongue, and told me I couldn't live in that house. I had to get out of there."

The house is in Diligent River just outside of Parrsboro, Nova Scotia.

Home From The War

The widow Mary Catherine McCabe was at the clothesline when she saw a young man in an army uniform. The young soldier stopped at Mary Catherine's gate, waved at her, and went inside the house. Mary Catherine fell to her knees in a weakened state. Her body went cold and stiff and a foreboding swept over her. It was her son Ethan, home from the war. She took a deep breath, got up, and slowly walked toward the open door. Questions cluttered her mind. Why was Ethan back from overseas and why would he go into the house first? Mary Catherine knew deep down in her heart and soul that when she stepped inside the kitchen, her son would not be there.

Late that evening Mary Catherine looked outside and watched an old man on a bicycle coming down the road. He wore a Western Union uniform. She heard his footsteps up the gravel driveway and then the knock on the door. She knew before opening the door what news the telegram contained.

Chapter Eight

Superstition, Fairies, and Folklore

Fairy Land

*T*his story is about the tiniest of all people, the fairies. Oh, they do abound, especially on Cape Breton Island.

You may be out in the countryside enjoying nature and hear voices but can't see anyone. You may believe that you're hearing things, but you're not. You're in little people country. The mysterious voices you hear may come from the strangest places—under large tree trunks, under gigantic boulders, and even in caves.

If by chance you come upon a large circle in the grass, that's a good sign there are fairies nearby and it would be wise not to linger too long. Not that fairies are mean, mind you, or want to harm you. Some of the little people, we're told, have a great sense of humour and they delight in seeing the surprised expression on the face of a mere mortal.

In The Tall Grass

*H*ave you ever heard the story of the Irish woodsman who found gold in the tall grass? If not, here t'is. The woodsman quickly and greedily filled his pockets with the bright, shiny stuff and was ready to hurry home when he thought of a way to find the exact spot when he returned for the rest of the gold. He picked up a large twig and drove it into the ground to mark the spot.

When he returned to get the rest of the gold, the whole meadow was filled with identical sticks. Needless to say, he had stumbled upon fairy gold and should have left well enough alone. Had he wished for some gold coins, then he may have been surprised to find a few pieces in his pockets when he arrived home. Fairies are like that. They grant wishes when folks are kind. Not greedy. That's what my Cape Breton friends tell me anyway.

Blarney, You Say

*T*here's something to be said for being in the right place at the right time. While my granddaughter Glenna Rizok and I were enjoying breakfast at the Westin Hotel in Halifax, I overheard the deep and familiar voice of the legendary Irish singer Tommy Makem. Tommy was having breakfast with his nephew Jimmy Sweeney, who is making a name for himself as a singer as well. I guess it's in the blood.

Well m'dears, after small talk was taken care of, my book became the topic of discussion. There's no Irishman on earth who'd pass up telling a ghostly tale or a story about the little people, and Jimmy Sweeney is no exception. He began telling my granddaughter and me the story that his grandfather, Tommy's father, had told him as a boy.

One black night Tommy's father and his buddies were taking a shortcut home when they were caught in fairy country. No matter how hard the friends tried, they could not find an opening in the long and tall hedges that were like iron fences. The men went around in circles most of the night. There was no use, they had to stay until the light of day to find their way out. But not Jimmy Sweeney's granddaddy. He knew how to outwit the fairies and beat them at their own game. He knew their secret—turn your coat inside out and out you go!

Jimmy smiled when he finished the story and so did his uncle Tommy Makem. Before we said our goodbyes, Jimmy told us that even today there are developers in Ireland who, in some regions of Erin, will not cut down trees or bulldoze land for fear of upsetting the little people. Ah, the Irish.

The Fairy Sisters

*B*ack in the mid-1800s, Bostonians and New Yorkers were amazed to see the smallest children on record appearing on stage in their cities. These children, famous in the United States, were virtually unknown in Nova Scotia, their birthplace.

Their names were Catherine, Victoria, and Dudley Foster. They were born in Chute's Cove, now Hampton. Their Annapolis Valley roots go back to the 1700s when the first Foster came to Nova Scotia from Massachusetts by way of England.

They were truly the little people. The sisters weighed just one pound at birth. At age ten, Cassie weighed 12 pounds and stood just 27 inches. At age three, Victoria weighed a mere 6 pounds and grew to only 17 inches. Most people who saw them considered them midgets. Not so, as medical records show that the bodies of the children were perfectly proportioned for their size.

The children's parents came down from Hampton Mountain to capitalize on the size of their children by showing them exclusively to American audiences. If it was to be a freak show, it would not be a Nova Scotian one. The girls were billed as The Fairy Sisters, headlining up and down the eastern seaboard of the United States.

In time, Victoria and Cassie returned to Hampton Mountain. Sadly, though, neither child reached their teen years. Dudley was born into the Foster family, but not until after the deaths of his sisters. Not only did he tour the United States, but Europe as well. While in London, Dudley was summoned to the palace where an anxious Queen Victoria waited to see this tiny Nova Scotian.

Like most Valley people, Margarete Wagner of O'Dell's Museum in Annapolis Royal never knew the children existed until she received a phone call from two New York ladies. The phone call came one hundred years after the deaths of Cassie and Victoria. The New York ladies were in possession of the girl's costumes and wanted them returned to the children's place of birth. Thanks to these ladies, visitors to the museum may see Cassie and Victoria's doll-like wardrobes. Also on display is the expensive miniature furniture that was made for the children by the Reid Furniture Company of Bridgetown, Nova Scotia.

Like his sisters, Dudley was not destined to live to an old age. Although death certificates have been located for Cassie and Victoria, records do not show one for Dudley. Be that as it may, he was laid to rest next to his tiny sisters in a cemetery on Hampton Mountain.

witchcraft

One of my all-time favourite stories reads like something out of a Harry Potter book, but was written long before the young wizard took to the air on his Nimbus Two Thousand. This traditional tale from Boutilier's Point, Nova Scotia appears in Helen Creighton's *Bluenose Magic* book. The child in all of us will love this little gem.

"When I was a boy and living with my grandfather, I used to help him. One day he wanted me to cut wood but I got contrary and decided that I'd run away. I started off and travelled along and it came on night in the woods and I saw a little house and thought I'd go in and stay all night.

"When I got in I looked around, there were three women there. I asked if they could keep me overnight, and they said, 'If we decide that, you'll go to bed and sleep all night; if you will do that, we'll put you up.' So I decided I'd do that.

"They put me to bed in a room by myself and they stayed in the kitchen. After awhile I pretended to be snorin' and one of the women came in and said, 'He's asleep.' The second one came in and said, 'He's asleep.' And the third one came in and said, 'He's sound asleep.'

"I watched through the crack in the wall and they had a bottle of grease. They greased themselves all over and said, 'Here we go, I and you and you and I,' and away they went, but I couldn't figure out where they went.

"I jumped out of bed and I found the bottle and I greased myself and I said, 'Here we go, I and you and you and I," and away I went. When I went out, they were sitting on the house roof and they said they'd have to take me with them. So they said, 'Here we go, I and you and you and I.'

"We had little round caps of cloth on our heads, and without them we couldn't go. We went right in the keyhole of a shop door, and the old women rummaged around and pulled things to pieces. One of them pulled the plug out of the molasses barrel and they said, 'Here we go, I and you and you and I,' but I couldn't go because I had lost my cap.

"The next day the man who owned the shop came in and asked me where I came from. I told him and he gave me to the police and the sentence was that I had to be hung.

"So they put me on the gallows and were just about to hang me when I saw a woman come flying through the air and she said, 'You ain't going to hang that fellow without his cap, are you?'

"They said no, so she put the cap on me head and she said, 'Here we go, I and you and you and I,' and I flew away with me cap on and the gallows around me neck."

A Headless Tale

W hile in Port Greville, Nova Scotia, I enjoyed listening to many stories of the good old days of sail. When I inquired about ghosts, whether on land or sea, I was asked if I was familiar with Ichabod Crane and the headless horseman story. I nodded in agreement and was proudly told that Port Greville had their own headless story—not a human, but a dog. The only problem was that no one knew the exact details of the story. Someone thought Dr. Helen Creighton had included the story in one of her many books, but they couldn't remember which one. I found the story on page 175 of *Bluenose Ghosts*. Their interpretation was not that much different from Dr. Creighton's. This is what they told me:

The headless dog was seen by a young seafaring lad by the familiar name of Hatfield from Port Greville. Young Hatfield would eventually command his own vessel. Hatfield and a shipmate were returning home from the sea and were about six miles from home in a place known as Ghost Hollow when they came upon the headless dog. Everyone knew it was foolhardy to be in Ghost Hollow at night. Be that as it may, when they'd gotten halfway up Mill Hill, a white dog suddenly appeared before their horse and wagon. The horse stopped dead in its tracks but Hatfield wasn't scared.

He sang out, "look at the dog!" and jumped off the wagon. He struck the dog with the whip, but the whip went straight through it. The dog then went under the wagon and disappeared. Young Hatfield travelled the Ghost Hollow Road many times after the incident, but never again did he encounter the headless dog.

The Vamp

*I*n the middle of the nineteenth century, a family living in the city of Moncton, New Brunswick, was, to say the least, most peculiar. Because of this peculiarity, they were given a wide berth by the rest of the community. Mothers told their children to stay away from the house down the lane, warning them that there were vampires and witches inside.

The home in question belonged to the Lutz family, which consisted of an aging mother and her eighteen-year-old daughter Rebecca. Since there is no record of the father, it's assumed he either died or deserted the family.

In the fall of that year, a mysterious illness claimed the life of Rebecca Lutz. She was denied a traditional burial by town and church leaders. As far as they were concerned, Rebecca was not going to have any chance to return to the land of the living, so they decided to bury her in a cement coffin. Some citizens shook their heads in disbelief while others held to the old ways.

Those who believed in the mystical and the occult had an uneasy feeling that a cement coffin was no guarantee of keeping a vampire down. Would Rebecca remain entombed forever?

Six months after Rebecca's death, her mother died as well. She ended up in a cement coffin next to her daughter.

I suppose those who believe in vampires and witches wonder if Rebecca and her mother are still prisoners of their cement homes. Or do they perhaps rise up with the first cluster of evening shadows to pass us on the streets of Moncton or sit across from us in coffee shops?

Stranger at the Gate

*D*eep in a January winter in Nova Scotia's Wentworth Valley, an old man painfully got up from his chair and, passing the window, he noticed a stranger standing down by the gate.

The old man waited for the figure to come knocking on his door, but he just stood there very tall, very erect, very rigid, and dressed entirely in black. The old man could feel his stare from the window.

It was snowing steadily, and a thought crossed his mind. It would be the Christian thing to invite the stranger inside where it was warm, but he couldn't just go out to talk to him. What if he had escaped from an asylum, or worse—what if he was from the hereafter? The old man remembered hearing stories about angels of death coming to claim what belonged to them.

"Best not to confront him," the old man thought, "best to leave well enough alone. The smart thing to do is wait him out. Anyway, with the wind picking up and the snow getting heavier, he'll be forced to leave."

He lit a lamp and made his way upstairs. The clock struck midnight as he got into bed. As his nightly ritual dictated, he read his Bible until he was too drowsy to read anymore. The only sounds that followed him into deep sleep were the howling winter winds and the ticking of the hall clock.

But another sound brought him back to consciousness; slow and deliberate footsteps making their way up the stairs. The old man sat up in bed cluthing his Bible to his heart. A terrible pain welled inside his chest as he watched the doorknob slowly turn.

It was his housekeeper who found him in the morning. The doctor said he died of natural causes—a heart attack, it was.

The Devil You Say

Down by the old train station in New Glasgow, Nova Scotia, there was at one time an old railway shack that was used for lunch breaks by trainmen. It was also a haven during storms and a place to pass the time playing poker.

According to Wayne MacAulay of New Glasgow, this terrifying story happened back in the early twenties. Wayne was a child on his father's knee when he first heard it.

Having just been paid, some railroaders headed for the shack where they gathered around an old table for a hand or two of poker. One young player was on a lucky streak and kept winning with a pair of deuces. He boasted that he was so hot he could even beat the devil.

A stranger entered the shack and asked if he could sit in. "Sure," they all replied. "We'll gladly take your money."

In no time at all, the stranger began winning every hand. No one likes a braggart or a poor loser, but our young friend with the former lucky streak was both. He threw down what he thought was a winning hand, sending the cards flying to the floor. Bending down to pick them up, he nearly fainted at a strange sight. Below the stranger's long black cloak were cloven hoofs! When the young man looked into his black, piercing eyes, a cold chill went through him. The stranger then turned into in a ball of fire, and went straight through the roof of the old shack. No matter how many times the hole was repaired, it would mysteriously appear again.

"The Devil you say," say I.